HONE

OR

WHAM, BAM, THANK YOU, MA'AM!

A SUPERHERO NOVELLA

David Perlmutter

Scarlet Leaf

2017

SCARLET LEAF

TORONTO ONTARIO CANADA

ISBN: 978-1-988827-33-9

Toronto, Canada

Table of Contents

Chapter One: The New Kid

The ride into town was about the only thing that would be normal about that day.

Of course, being a newly minted superhero, I knew I wouldn't be having any more "normal" days, with all my new challenges and responsibilities. You never know when trouble's going to loom, y'know.

Since you're from out of town, you may not have heard of me before. So, allow me to introduce myself.

For the first eight years of my life, I was just plain old Olivia Thrift, from Headingley, Manitoba, just outside of Winnipeg. A normal girl in a normal town, somebody who kept mostly to herself, with few friends. Other than my best one, Dixon Wells, whom I've known since before we both had teeth. But even he didn't have time for me all the time. And my parents have to commute really deep into Winnipeg for work, so they're not always around or up and about when I need them. So, there's been a fair bit of time in my life when I was a total latchkey kid, alone with my books and the TV.

That's how my being a superhero came about. The animated ones on TV became my favorites, and then my older cousin Ella Thrift, who's the biggest fan-girl in the universe, got me into the comics. Especially now that there's a *lot* more women and girls in the superhero biz than there used to be. Of course, I didn't know then that I would become *friends* with them, let alone breathe the same air as any of them. Let *further* alone that I'd actually be part of an epic, cataclysmic adventure with them. If you'd told me that a couple of years ago I'd be doing that, I would have thought you were *out* of your gourd.

But I *did* become a superhero, and it *did* happen. But, first, you need to know *how* I became who I am now for this to make any sense to you.

*

I had just finished watching the tube one night, when I thought I heard somebody calling my name from within the set as the picture went dead. I crept forward, but, just before I got to the screen, a ghost appeared and startled the living daylights out of me, and I jumped back.

I'd had a couple of glasses of ginger ale that night, which I didn't normally do, and my head was a little dizzy. So, I wasn't sure if I was imagining this or not. Like a goof, I asked it:

"Are you for *real*?"

To my great surprise, it said, "Yes".

Actually, "it" was a "he", so I should call him that instead. I'm all about giving respect when it's deserved or earned. And he earned mine right away.

His name was Lightsound, and he was and is a deity who resides in all communication devices through which information is transmitted. Digital ones, mostly, since that's most of what they are now, anyway.

So, again like a goof, I asked him again:

"You mean you're from the telephone company?"

"No," he said, clearly and patiently, but without any annoyance whatsoever.

He was an alien being sent to Earth to do good deeds, who happened to reside where he did because it was the only way he could avoid being attacked and killed by "my" outside world. And he had chosen to reveal himself to me because he wished to do for me one of his good deeds.

"Me?" I asked. "What did I possibly do to deserve something like that? I'm not special."

He contradicted me. He noted my strong interest in super-heroics, and I didn't deny it. And then he noted a long list of things I had done in and around my home that qualified me for superhero status (in his eyes, anyway). I attribute that more to being a faithful Spark, Brownie and Girl Guide than anything else. As well as the many times I've come to my best friend's aid when he needed it. Such as when I got into a vicious scrap with a bigger girl to protect Dixon from her bullying. I won the fight, but ended up getting detention for a whole week because of it. Because my hypocrite teacher of the moment thought that "girls should know better than to fight" when he let the boys get away with it all the time. Who says life is fair?

But Dixon appreciated it, as he always does when I assist him in any way. He thinks I can fight very well, and never adds "for a girl" to it, unlike some people. He's always glad if somebody stands up for him, boy or girl, because his being so short by guy standards makes it harder for him to defend himself by himself. I'm glad he's on my side.

Anyway, I had forgotten all of that, as well as the various animals I helped out if they were stuck in a tree or fell out of their nest trying to learn how to fly. Not that many - Headingley's very small - but Lightsound had somehow seen all of this and made a mental note of it all. And now, because I admired superheroes so much, he wanted to make me one, in turn.

"So how are you going to do that?" I asked, still trying to come to terms with a dream that had the potential to come true. "Are you going to....?"

Before I could say any more, he shaped hands from his ethereal, non-corporeal form and put them on my arms. Then I got shocked with enough electricity to kill an elephant. Somehow, I survived, but I fell to the ground. Lightsound stood protectively over me until the charge faded, which happened soon afterwards.

"What...did you...*do*...to me?" I said, once I regained consciousness, with a headache. "I feel so..."

"The negative feelings will pass," he said. "You will begin to pulsate with strength and speed greater than anyone else your age. As well as a higher level of intelligence. The headache you feel is your brain expanding."

But he said I didn't have to be super all the time if I didn't want to. A great relief to me, because I know full well what an albatross being super 24-7 can be. He told me I could use key words to cue him for when I wanted to super up and power down. So, I picked "Fantastic!" to cue my powers, using a jump in the air as a visual punctuation mark, and "Done!" for when I wanted to quit. Then he zapped up a uniform for my superhero identity, partially based on the pajamas I was wearing at the time.

(That's my old one, not the one I have on now. Long story, but you'll hear all of it soon.)

So, that's why I call myself Captain Fantastic when I'm a superhero. Otherwise, I'm just plain old Olivia.

The only condition Lightsound gave me for having my powers was that I show other kids the way they could unlock their potential the way he did mine. By translating their deepest mental desires into physical realities. Hence those famous kids-only seminars I hold once in a while. If they'll let me, that is.

Then he left, saying all I needed to do to contact him was call his name, and he'd be there. Swell guy.

Anyhow, I'm sorry if I wasted your time filling in my life story, but, like I said, the rest of what happened to me, then won't make a lot of sense to you if I don't do that first.

And speaking of the rest of the story....

Chapter Two: The Role Model

I keep my identities separate from each other, for the most part. The only one who knows the truth besides me and Lightsound is Dixon. Only because he saw me exercising my super strength on an abandoned piano in a junkyard as Captain Fantastic, and called out to me as Olivia.

After I ran over and shushed him (although there was no one else there to hear him), I told him what had happened. He believed it, entirely. Especially when I told him I'd do to him what I did to the piano if he blabbed and ratted me out. Which he also believed entirely - and nervously. Although both of us know he wouldn't blab and I wouldn't lay a finger on him for real, us being pals.

He's not the adventurous type, so, when I offered him the chance to sidekick, he said he'd rather be my PR man, and so I let him do my PR. One less straw on my back.

My Mom and Dad, now, that's different. She teaches English lit at U of M, and would just dismiss what happened to me as a tall tale on my part that I made up, knowing her. He's a guard at the jail in Headingley, and doesn't care for fantasy as he deals with reality every day. All he wants out of me is for me not to end up like any of the women he supervises, who are almost all bad news.

If only he knew…

Either way, no dice telling them the truth. So, when it came time for me to attend my first Canadian Consortium of Superheroines convention, which was, fortuitously being held in Winnipeg that year, I had to tell Mom a little while lie and say that I was participating in an all-day elementary school John Dos Passos seminar.

She agreed to drive me to the Millennium Library, where the convention was being held, although she probably wondered why and I and the other kids would waste an entire day talking about an author even she had trouble understanding.

So, I got out of the car, said goodbye, and walked down Graham Avenue towards the Library entrance. The convention program was pasted onto one of the windows of the entrance, and I looked it over. I nearly screamed with delight when I saw who the keynote speakers were.

The Suckerpunch Girls!

I'd worshipped them on TV for years, and *now*…. but somehow I managed not to embarrass myself.

For a millisecond, and then it became harder not to do it.

When I realized that the one superheroine I loved above all others - since she was a fellow Manitoban especially - was standing mere inches away from me, looking at the same ad.

MUSCLE GIRL *HERSELF*!

I didn't recognize her immediately, 'cause she was out of uniform, in her civvies. But there was no way she could completely disguise that uniquely powerful body of hers in that skirt and sweater. Nor could she completely disguise her all-seeing electric blue eyes, or her ever-bouncy, pig-tailed blonde hair. She plays her beauty down a lot herself. But she's *gorgeous.*

Not that I'm.... you know...

I'm just *saying*....

Well, you know how it is when you meet a celebrity you adore. How can you possibly tell them you love them in a cool, calm and collected way? When you're so awestruck that even the most articulate of us become tongue-tied morons in their very presence? No wonder so many of them don't even *care* about their fans!

Not that MG's like that, of course. One thing I admire about her above anything else is that, despite having an intellect even greater than mine, she is always and completely both humble about her unique gifts, and honest in her instant and direct assessments of events and people.

Thus, more than anyone else, she is my role model as a supe. So, naturally, I feared embarrassing myself in front of her in particular, and possibly putting her off me based on only her first impression of me. Which, given her storied past, would be a bad thing for me. Especially if I was an evil being who had hurt her in the past. Then she'll show you no mercy whatsoever.

Muscle Girl has never shied away from talking about her difficult past and how she has triumphed over it to achieve success. How she was a bullied weakling as a little kid, on a distant planet far from Earth. How she and her family had to flee that planet as beleaguered political refugees to settle here. How she gained her incredible strength, speed, agility and ability to fly due to the gravitational differences between her origin planet and Earth, just like the immortal Superman himself.

Her remarkable adventures, full of remarkable rescues, escapes and unparalleled bravery and selflessness, have already made her the stuff of legend, if only just here in Canada. As are her knock-out, drag-down battles with her mean and evil nemesis, Petra O'Leum, the Girl Made of Rock. Who's not only her equal in speed and strength, having come from the same planet as MG, but wealthy, arrogant and smart enough to make both of us look like idiots.

Petra used her wild card abilities to defeat MG in battle in their first fight, and MG was so disillusioned that she nearly gave up the game for good. Fortunately, Cerberus, the mightiest puppy in the universe, was willing and able to take her under her wing and show her exactly what she needed to do to defeat Petra, and therefore restored her confidence enough for her to come back in from the cold.

Afterwards, another, larger problem inspired the two of them to form the International League of Girls with Guns (in this case, muscles, not firearms, which they all despise) with the three heroines they met combatting that crisis.

Candy Girl, the Titan of Teens, whose courage, strength and agility confronting evil is only stopped when her Asperger's syndrome challenged brain saps her confidence, as it is wont to do some times.

Power Bunny, a kick-ass female rabbit heroine from Anthropomorph, where all the world's animated cartoon characters hail from, and with both the daring and the humor to prove that well and often.

And the Brat, a half-mechanical, half-organic alien resembling a female toddler, but much more bad-ass than her external appearance might suggest.

Together, they are nearly as unstoppable as when they are working their beats alone. When they aren't getting on each other's nerves sometimes, which is inevitable in these kinds of situations. Just ask me and Dixon when it happens to us.

God, I would *love* to play a hand with them at the poker games they regularly play together at their headquarters, a combination club house and space station just off of Earth's orbit. If only I knew anything about playing cards....

Anyway, MG's said all this in her own stories and interviews better than I can here in summary. Really worth seeking out. And the ILGWG stories are *classics....*

Darn it! I'm turning into Ella. Get it *together*, Thrift!

The point is, I was standing close enough to her that I could actually *touch* her. And I might have, had she not turned around and faced me. With that benign but hypnotic stare that can reduce her enemies to jelly, and can utterly entrance any boy her age who first locks eyes with her in a single moment. As if she were a gorgon who had just turned him to stone.

"Why don't you take a picture?" she asked, in that impish tomboy voice of hers that is both innocent and commanding at the same time. "It'll *last* longer."

I didn't know what to say at first. Was she mad at me for violating her privacy? What might she do to me as punishment? Would I, perhaps, have to defend myself from her wrath, even though I was more than capable of answering hers with my own if need be?

But then, I realized that she wasn't being serious. Just funny and clever like she is, and I only wish I could be. Her wit is as legendary and disarming as the rest of her, since only her most hated enemies won't laugh when she cracks a good joke. And I wasn't an enemy, so I started laughing.

She responded to my laughter by laughing herself.

The ice had been broken!

"Hi, Olivia," she said, patting my shoulder. "Good to see you. At last."

Then I got nervous again.

"You *know* who I *am*?" I asked.

"We all know who we "really" are in this business, girlfriend, "she said, with her well-known bluntness. "That was why you had to give us information about your "real" name and identity when you applied for membership. Remember? But don't worry. We all keep each other's secrets, and never blab about them to each other besides ourselves. That's the only way we can keep them safe. So, we can do our jobs without people trying to connect the dots between our identities, the way Lois Lane is always trying to find the truth about Superman. We don't need that salt on our tails in the real world. Except on the occasions when you let a silent partner in the game, like you did with your pal. Pretty smart move on your part there."

"Thank you, Muscle Girl. I...."

Her face contorted into a resentful glare for a moment. But only a moment, thankfully.

"Please! It's only the outside world that calls me that- most of the time. My pals all call me Gerda." (Gerda Munsinger is her secret identity.) "I called *you* Olivia, *not* Captain Fantastic. So, could you please show me the same courtesy, if you don't *mind*?"

I'm sorry…. Gerda…."

"Don't be so apologetic. You aren't like that when you fight with your enemies, after all."

"So you know about…my whole career….so far?"

"Well, as a dispassionate observer in this get-up, anyway. The League and I were off-planet when you made your debut. Probably, it was on one of the nights when we play cards. I'm not sure. We keep a close eye on things across the whole universe in the station for when we're needed, but not on the nights when it's game on. But all the blogs and websites I follow for professional reasons were buzzing about you when I got back, and all of them seemed to speculate on what it might mean for me. Negative things, mostly, knowing a lot of them like I do. Like how you were gunning to replace me, the way a young punk gunslinger from the Wild West wanted to kill all the guys who were better than him. But most of those people are just cranks who don't know any better. 'Cause they just *watch* people like us do our job all day, and don't even try to do it themselves. Still, I knew I had to make sure that I kept my game tight in case our paths crossed in a negative way, rather than a positive way like now. If the two of us ever decided to drop the gloves on each other, for any reason, I doubt Winnipeg would be still be standing, and one of us would end up dead. And the other would carry the guilt of that murder on their conscience the rest of her life.

"But you don't deserve to have that happen to you, Olivia. Not in the slightest. You're just like me, after all. A good girl. But a good girl can only take so much before she feels the need to strike against the beings that hurt her. Even the ones who wound her deep, but unintentionally. I've been there. And I'm sure you have been, too. So, we need to help each other and not hurt each other. Especially when one of us can't do it alone, which happens more often than you think. Hence the League, for instance."

"I'm glad you don't think of me as a rival, or, worse, a pretender to your throne, Gerda," I answered. "I mean, given how some of the people in this business can be, I was worried that, when and if I met you in person, you would be...?"

"Jealous?" she finished. "Or bitchy? Or *worse*? You're thinking of the *adults*, kid. And *just* them, thankfully. We pre-teen and teenage girls, in particular, *help* each other. Because we *need* to. I don't need to tell you about all the crap we in particular have to deal with. Girls our age, or older- or even younger- who are jealous of or otherwise resentful of us and want to kill us, and *can*. Because they're just as strong and fast and et cetera as we are. Or even *stronger*. And their *tongues* are as sharp and as wounding as any physical weapon they could use against us. Like that of my "pal" Petra O'Leum, for example.

"Boy enemies can be even worse. You've got two strikes against you there instead of one. Not only have you crushed his pride by being better than him, but you've also done it while being "merely" a girl, besides. So, he wants you gone twice as much as any girl does in the same boat. And he can do things to you girls can't, or won't, or don't, and doesn't mind telling you that to your face if he thinks you're not a crybaby and can "handle" it. But it's even better showing him he's mistaken than it is clipping a girl hater's wings.

"And don't get me started on those showboating adults. It doesn't matter that they were doing this long before you and I were born, and they probably taught you and I and everyone else in this business how to do it, and well. The people who print their comics and make their movies nowadays think it's much more *fun* to see them rip on *each other* instead of on the bad guys, and wail and thrash about and cry crocodile tears about what a "hard" life they have. Then, they make it appear that we're all *like* that, implicitly, and give us all a bad name by doing it. They invented most of that stuff to sell their theater tickets and the rest of their merchandise to stupid rubes who don't know what kind of rip-offs they are and never will. Which is why they keep coming back for more of the same. All that it is and it ever will be is a *lie*, in comparison to how we *actually* live and conduct our duties. In other words- *BUNK*!"

She used her full mighty Muscle Girl voice on that last word, rather than the more modest, "girlish" one she usually uses as Gerda. So, that got some stares for a minute from other people, but they let it go.

"Are you okay, Gerda?" I asked.

"Yeah," she smiled. "But you know what it's like having a public forum, but having to be squeaky clean all the time because they don't *expect* you to swear, or leer, or bark an order at them, or do anything else that's not "lady-like". Don't you?"

"You're preaching to the choir."

"Okay. Well, the point I was making with that rant was that, although we may both very well be the heavyweight champion of our physical and metaphysical weight class, there's no point in us being enemies. The Muscle Girl/Captain Fantastic cage match the press seems to want- particularly the men- is not going to happen if we can help it. We're going to be friends, and only that. That is, if you want to be my friend. Far be it from me to force you to be pals with me - that's not my style at all. But it'd be much better for both of us than the other way, believe me."

I utterly screamed with joy inside. But, on the outside, I just said:

"Of course. Nothing would make me feel happier."

"*That's* a relief," she said, as her powerful hand shook mine to seal it. "I feel the same way. Manitoba is big enough for more than one super-powered cop on the beat. So, from now on, the stuff you handle is the stuff I don't need to worry about, and vice versa. Unless either of us can't deal with it alone, of course."

"Definitely."

"We better get inside. The out-of-town girls will be coming down here from the Marlborough any minute now. And I think they'll be as glad to meet and befriend you as I've been. Any new blood is good blood. We need all the help we can get."

Chapter Three: The Convention

Sure enough, they began coming up the street just as Gerda finished talking.

To look at us, we didn't look much like superheroes. We only wear our uniforms on duty, of course, and we were all in our civvies.

Gerda and I were a little dressed up in comparison to the others, in her sweater and skirt and my dress. They were all about casual clothes. Helps when you need to change your clothes and ID quickly, they all agreed. You just ripped off the externals when you went into battle. Probably the way I would have done it if I didn't have my magic words.

Let me put it this way. You get a group of girls aged between eight and twelve together, without adult supervision of any kind (none of us need or want it, anyway), and the last thing you'd think we were was superheroes from different regions of Canada, the way we were gabbing and carrying-on as if it was the only thing we knew how to do.

But that's how it was. We're the kids protecting you from evil, Canada. You don't know it, most of you. As it should be. But it's perfectly true.

As my colleagues' reputations all preceded them extensively, as had Gerda's, I was as awestruck meeting them as I had been her initially. But each of them put me at ease the same way she has, since, unlike our many enemies, we don't have a jealous bone in any of our bodies.

It helped greatly that we had things in common with each other we only just discovered then.

For starters, there was Manon Rheaume, better known in her native Quebec, and particularly her native Montreal, as *Superflic*. She was thrilled to know that my Mom's family originally came from France, way before her or my time. I protested that I was nowhere near as fluent in French as she so obviously was, but she was glad to know that I had learned *some* of that language.

"Gerda, though," she said to me, "she speaks Joual like she grew up in the shadow of Mount Royal, same as I did. *Tabarnache*! Any Anglo girl that pick it up that quickly you gotta respect!"

And Manon respects her own heritage. That's for sure. We all carried snapshots of ourselves in our work duds to see what we looked like in them, because we didn't think- then that we'd have to do any actual heavy lifting during the convention.

Manon dresses in a Montreal Canadiens jersey and short pants, like she was actually playing hockey for them, although the stylized "C" in the center was replaced by an equally stylized "S". Fittingly, she's played hockey herself for a number of years, and tends to do her heroics in the same rough-and-tumble manner some players do their careers.

But any immortality that might imply is canceled out by her being a good Catholic, as most *Quebecois* people are. That, in fact, was how she became a hero in the first place, not unlike my experience with Lightsound, but in a religious way.

In a difficult time in her life, she prayed for guidance, and was rewarded by being able to become the heroine she wanted to be whenever she prays it be so in the future.

It will also help, as she joked, whenever it may be that the "Habs" may sue her for violating their copyright so blatantly!

With Quinn O'Regan, the Newfie Bullet, on the other hand, it was simply that we were both redheads.

"Anuther red'ead- at last!" she drawled, in her home island's distinctive patois. "I was begin'in to t'ink I was the only one 'ere who weren't yellow nor black on top."

Quinn, like Manon, comes from a Catholic background, but, unlike her, doesn't put much faith in the Church. Her family once had to deal with some real nasty priests who ran an orphanage there, and weren't exactly kind to the kids.

Those scars still run deep down the whole Rock's line. But she doesn't hold that against Manon, because they both know that what happened in the past wasn't either of their faults, and that's no reason for their strong friendship to suffer.

It helps that Quinn is every bit the athlete herself. She credits her prowess on court and field, along with her giant-by-little-girl-standards size, with giving her the confidence, strength and agility she employs on a regular basis as her heroic identity- named for the mighty train that used to crisscross all of Newfoundland- in and around her native St. John's.

"Mind ya," she told me, "doin' it the natural way, without intervention from higher powers, has its disadvantages. I ain't bulletproof, and, for that alone, I can't be nearly as foolhardy as some of our lot can be. Although I also can't be entirely as brave on that score, either."

So, too, does Candas Dorsey, the Angel of the Tar Sands, who covers the parts of the Prairies that don't include Manitoba. She wishes she could fly as much as Quinn wishes she was bulletproof, and for the same reason: it would make her job a lot easier to do.

While most of us could be considered spiritual children of Superman (and, in my case, the old non-female Captain Marvel from the 1940s), Candas uses Batman as her spiritual guide. They're both wealthy, and both prefer using weapons to fists because they're mortal and not super-powered. Also, because that's the only way to even the score in those situations. Plus, Candas wears a spooky-looking cowl on duty, whereas the rest of us keep our faces bare.

However, Candas as a person is more like how Batman was when Adam West was playing him, and not any of the stoic but insensitive guys who have played him since then. She doesn't take herself too seriously, and, like Gerda and me, believes wholeheartedly in giving back to her community and providing assistance to her friends when they need it. But not to her enemies, of course.

The newest member of the group, besides me, is Anna Robertson, better known as the Raven. She's an Indigenous girl from Ontario's Six Nations reserve.

Her fascination with the culture and lore of her Mohawk and Iroquois ancestors led her, through study and practice, to become a heroine by practicing the arts of shape-shifting and ghost walking to turn herself into anything she needed to become in order to set things right if she thought they were bad.

Her favorite form, of course, is the animal she chose to call herself after, for she admires the heroic role it has played in her people's culture.

Anna has been working her craft for a couple of years, but it's only been recently that she joined the Consortium. Like many of her people, she has suffered psychologically from the stinging racism and condescension white Canadians have often heaped upon them in the past.

She was afraid that, because that the rest of us are Caucasian, we would view her the same way. Which is *ridiculous*. When her acceptance was sent out, Gerda made it a point to tell her that with her usual combination of friendliness, bluntness and wit.

That broke the ice as swiftly as did between her and me and the rest of the group. Her people have enough difficulty with their lives as we have ours, and we sympathize with them completely due to that.

Anna was really into what I was doing, it turned out. Particularly my public speaking seminars.

"I need to do that on the reserve," she said. "On *all* of them, actually. Everybody's hurting there now. Can you show me how to put together one of those presentation things?"

"You bet," I said. "We got to spread this empowerment message as far and as wide as we can to the people who need it. Yours definitely included."

So, after coming there with no friends of my own gender at all, I ended up leaving with five. Not a bad day's work.

But things were just getting started.

*

After about a half an hour of gabbing, mostly getting to know each other, but including a spirited but good-natured debate between Manon and Quinn about which of them had *really* won the swimming race they'd had the previous night in the Marlborough pool, Gerda called us to attention to get the formal part of the event over with.

That surprised us, as our guest speakers had not even appeared yet. So, I asked Gerda what was up.

"They're not coming," she said, bluntly.

Boy, did that take the wind out of our sails! We stood there with our mouths wide open, like turkeys in the rain.

"What happened?" I said.

"Did they break up?" Quinn asked.

"Are they sick?" Manon said.

"They didn't decide to go bad, did they?" inquired Candas.

"Please don't tell me that they went missing," shouted Anna. "Or that they were murdered!"

"Nothing like that," Gerda said. "It's a legal matter, babies."

"Legal?" I asked.

"Uh huh," said Gerda.

"They're not defendants in a trial, are they?" Candas asked.

"It's not a trial, Candas," Gerda reported. "It's a lawsuit."

"Lawsuit?" I repeated. "Who would want to sue them? Other than their enemies, I mean."

"*They* are the ones suing Moving Drawings Studios," Gerda answered.

"The company that produced their show back in the day?" I continued. "Why would they do that?"

"Because said entity," Gerda growled, contemptuously, "has had the singular temerity to revive their program and produce a new version of it. Without their *consent*. And, even worse, they kept them in the dark about it until after they produced enough episodes with the *clones* replacing them for *a whole season. At least*."

"WHAT?"

We must have gotten everyone attention's in the whole library with that one collective cry of outrage, though only for a moment. But we didn't care. Because our collective heroines and role models were being threatened by something we had all feared might happened one day. That their reputations - nay, their very existence - as we knew and loved them were being threatened. By fakes pretending to be them, and jerks in the boardroom who didn't think about them except as moving dollar signs! Which often happens when you get caught in the corporate machine the way they unfortunately did.

"The company assumes - *falsely*, of course," Gerda continued, "that, when they signed the contract with them to have their adventures filmed in the first place, they signed away legal control over the use of their name, their images and their very identities as individuals. They disagree, violently, as they should, because that's a crock. I'm sure they would have wanted to fly through the executive offices of Moving Drawings and kill every person there that they saw, given how furious about it they were when I talked to them on the phone last night when they gave their regrets. But that's not how they or any of us conduct our affairs, by any means. And you can't fight a corporation on the streets, anyway, because, *regardless* of what the courts may say, they are not individuals. So, that's where they're taking their fight - the courts. The paperwork's just been filed, and they're waiting to give their depositions. If they leave Townsberg, they forfeit the right to sue. So, that's why they're not here."

We were crestfallen.

"If it's any consolation, ladies," Gerda concluded, "I'm as upset about this as you are. But they want us to go ahead with our plans, like nothing happened, because that's the only mature way we can respond to this. I imagine that Nelvana would probably say the same thing if she were still here and with us. So, let's do just that."

She meant Nelvana of the Northern Lights - the very first Canadian super-heroine, from way back in the 1940s, and the founder of the Consortium. We all mumbled her name softly, and Manon crossed herself, as we went up to the Carol Shields Auditorium for the main part of the meeting.

*

So, having been deprived of our keynote, we went right into our business.

Actually, "business" is pushing it. It was more like us swapping tales about our most recent adventures.

Gerda had a slight advantage over us, having had ones both on her own and with the League, but, to be fair to the rest of us, she only explained the solo ones.

Being as Anna and I were more recent in joining, we couldn't contribute as much to the discussion as the others. So, we mostly listened rather than talking. Although, when we were asked to explain ourselves, we made sure to talk about the things that had happened to us that really counted.

However, the fun vanished from the room quickly, when Anna explained that she had been recently been forced to fight off a group of similarly looking beings who had been intent on turning Six Nations into a Disney-style resort without the band council's consent. Or even its very knowledge.

When she said that, the rest of us gasped in horror. And the usually very fearless Gerda turned chalk white. Obviously, this was something bad.

Only I didn't know what it was.

"Who are these guys?" I asked, naively. "And why are they bad?"

"They're known as the Merch," said Gerda, rapidly regaining her composure. "We don't have to explain everything bad they've done, all over the universe. You'd need an entire set of the Encyclopedia Britannica to do that."

"I just need the Coles Notes version," I said. "Did they just come on the block?"

"Hardly. But Anna's account marks the first time they've tried to do their shell games on Earth. If their reputation precedes them as it does, the whole planet is in trouble. And we, ladies, are the only ones who are going to be able to stop them!"

Almost on cue, we all gasped again. But I still didn't get all of it.

"This is confusing," I admitted. "I don't understand...."

"You *should*," Anna snapped at me. "How would you like to have decisions about whether you *lived* or *died* made *without* you even there?" She started crying. "That's how my whole *life* has been."

"Oh, Anna," I said, tearing up myself and embracing her. "I didn't mean to set you off like that. You know that all of us want to..."

"I know," Anna responded, as we dried our eyes with Kleenex Gerda gave us. "But it's so hard to find genuine kindness nowadays. People say they want to help you, and then they betray you behind your back. For no good reason."

"Yeah," agreed Candas. "It's like that old Motown song. 'Smiling faces sometimes pretend to be your friend'. *Especially* when you have superpowers and/or do heroic deeds."

"Some folks is just like that, though," Quinn said, as she grit her teeth. "My enemies, f'r example."

"And mine," added Manon. "Lotta folk think they can take advantage of us just 'cause we're girls. Like we were just fresh from the nipples of our *mamans*. *Idiotes*!"

"But the worst ones," said Gerda, "are a certain class of men who never got the message that women and girls are people. With *feelings*. That they don't even *bother* to understand. They ignore the fact that we have - or, in our case, will have in a few years - the right to vote, own property and have careers of our choosing the same as them. They just want us to shut up and do what they tell us to do, and then, when we grow up, turn us into "docile" helpmates and baby factories! And some sickos among them can't even wait until we become legal adults before they decide to make "women" of us!"

"You said it, Gerda," Candas said. "Even here, in this supposedly progressive-minded place, there are men with warped minds who can only think of girls like us as walking pieces of ass and treat us accordingly."

She paused, and looked at all of us apologetically.

"I'm sorry if I offended you," she said. "It's just that sometimes I have to see some real bad stuff."

"No need," I put in. "My dad the jail guard tells me about some of what the ladies he looks over have done. So, I won't dare to do them myself."

"Montreal's no paradise that way," said Manon.

"Neither is St. John's," added Quinn.

"For every horror story you might have seen in the cities of the Prairies, Candas," Anna declared, glumly, "I'll match you one just as bad on the reserves. You all know now about those barbaric residential schools, and how they tried to obliterate my people's independence, integrity, traditions, history and free will, thanks to the work of the Truth and Reconciliation Committee. So, I'm sure you have a better sense of what we were suffering through then and still have to deal with now, don't you?"

We all nodded.

"I did a paper at school on them," I said. "They were just as bad as the Holocaust, or Stalin's Gulags. Maybe even worse."

"Well, Olivia," Anna continued, as she faced me in particular, "you asked before what was so bad about the Merch. Here it is. They think of us human beings only as commodities to be bought or sold, like shoes or blankets. And they intend to do that with all the peoples of Earth, and its animals, and its natural resources. Once they lock us all up and away in conditions that make the residential schools look like a Sunday picnic."

"That's... *outrageous*!" I answered. "We shouldn't *stand* for that!"

"Then you know how I felt when I learned about their plans to buy and sell me and my people and all our property behind our backs. Exactly!"

"Well, they aren't going to get away with it as long as we live or breathe. If they know what's *good* for them, they won't even try to fool with us!" Gerda shouted. She struck the table with her fist so hard that the whole table wobbled in response to feeling her superhuman strength at full power. "And if they don't - and I suspect given who and what they are, they don't - we have to give 'em *what for*, don't we?"

The rest of us answered loudly in agreement.

"Excellent," said Gerda. "We all agree that we should...."

She was cut off by a massive reverberation which shook the Library to its very foundation. What Gerda had just done to the table, somebody was now trying to do to the whole building.

With us and the Library's patrons and staff still inside, and seemingly helpless.

Chapter Four: The Villain

"Hurry!" Gerda ordered. "Get into your uniforms, and quickly! We gotta stop this in its tracks before they blame us for *causing* it!"

"Would they *dare* to do that?" I said, incensed, as the other girls rushed to the nearest ladies' washroom to change, to Gerda before she joined them.

"You better *know* it, kid," she replied.

"But we're….heroines! How could they….?"

"Yeah, I know. The license plate says 'Friendly Manitoba'. But even friendliness has its limits. You wreck somebody's whole city, even protecting it from evil, and some folks find it very hard to forgive you."

"That's….*prejudice*!"

"You can get as mad as you want about it, Olivia. But I know as well as any of us that that is just the way it is here on the ground. It's not going to change. Not overnight, anyway. So, we just need to keep our upper lips stiff and deal with it."

"But…."

"Just say your magic word and do your *job*, okay? That's all you can do. You can't control what other people think about you, just like you can't when you're just a mortal. And unless you think otherwise, you better *shut up and drink your milk*!" She rushed out. "Meet you out front."

So I took her advice. I jumped up in the air, and shouted:

"FANTASTIC!"

Just like that, Olivia Thrift was gone. Then Captain Fantastic was, too.

*

Those of us could fly met in the air, while the others gathered on the ground. I had my aforementioned old suit on, and Manon her aforementioned one as well. Quinn wore her blue one-piece bathing suit with the majestic flag of Newfoundland and Labrador in its center. Candas was all in black, from her hair to her shoes, with her aforementioned cowl over her head and her equally black eyes serious as cancer beneath. Anna, meanwhile, had stripped off the hoodie she came in to reveal a silkscreened T-shirt image of a gigantic raven that seemed to burst right out of her chest.

And Gerda, of course, was in the magnificent duds as she wears as Muscle Girl, in all her glory. The main body of the suit was pink, but she wore panties and a cape that were whiter than the driven snow, and had her monogram stamped on the chest and cape in gold. Along with silver boots that have lifts in them, that allowed her to be slightly taller as MG than she was as Gerda. Further assuring everyone who didn't know the truth that they were not the same person. At *all*.

We were all gathered now in the Park just outside of the Library and named for it. Facing the giant wall of plate glass cut into square windows that marks the northern border of the facility. Which, due to current events, was starting to shed that glass, and was likely to have its foundation further compromised if the metal skeleton of that wall gave way under the enormous power being asserted on it.

Unless we did something. Fortunately, Gerda, with her clever mind, had already figured out what to do.

"Everyone take the nearest corner of the wall you can reach," she said. "And *put everything you got* against it! Don't flinch, or anything like that. Even if the glass breaks on or around you and hurts you. That we can take. What we can't take is getting fingered for this- for any reason. Let's get it done, ladies!"

And we did.

Here's what happened:

The Newfie Bullet rushed over to the left side of southern part of the wall and threw her body on it. She got that part to stop wobbling with a great exertion. However, when she did that, the glass exploded, and shards went into her naked arms and legs. And since she's neither bulletproof nor otherwise invulnerable, she felt a lot of pain.

"JESUS, MARY AND *JOSEPH*!" she screeched.

But she still held on.

Superflic went over to the right side of the southern part and held onto it in the same fashion as the Bullet. And got breaking glass exploding into her body, too, for all her trouble.

"*TABERNACHE*!" she shouted. "*Mes yeux*!"

But she, too, still held on.

The Angel of the Tar Sands measured the distance between where she was on the ground and the roof of the Library mentally. Then she whipped out a grappling hook, fired it right on the roof, and climbed up the rope she'd attached to it beforehand to the middle of the glass grid. That, fortunately for her, had already lost most of its glass. No shrapnel in the body this time, but she would have been protected from most of that by her sweatshirt and pants. She started holding on, too, although she isn't nearly as strong as the rest of us combined.

I hit the left upper right hand corner. One corner of the right hand side broke just as I approached it, and I had to duck the shrapnel as it came for me. Then I grabbed the metal frame of the wall and pulled on it with all the strength I had, as instructed.

Muscle Girl went to the left upper corner. She was braver than I was in dealing with the glass. Windows exploded in front of her, too. But she was able to get it to bounce off her mighty chest like it was nothing at all. She's the most experienced of us, and the most fearless, so I wasn't surprised she used her body to laugh in the face of danger like that. When she smacked herself against her assigned corner and applied her powerful muscles to the wall, with a combination loud yell and grunt, I prayed that our labour would soon end.

However, even our combined might wasn't enough to stop the wobbling, it seemed. As symbolized when the Angel of the Tar Sands lost her grip and fell back down to the ground.

"CANDAS!" I shouted, in horror, on glancing to see it.

"No worries," she shouted up to us, over the din. "I'll deal. Hey- where's Anna?"

At that moment, an enormous grizzly bear- female, of course- emerged directly behind the Angel, and roared. Candas turned around and shrieked in fear.

"Candas, it's me!" the bear said. "Anna!"

"Wow!" Candas said, in admiration. "You really are a shape-shifter, aren't you?"

"Darn right I am," said the Anna-bear. "I know exactly what kind of animals I can turn into, especially when people need my help. And right now, we need the kind of strength that only a bear has to get out of this fix. Because there's no animal in the forest nobler- or more powerful- than the BEAR!"

That being said, the Anna-bear threw itself where the Angel of the Tar Sands had just fallen from, uttering a roar of defiance as its paws grasped the foundation and threw its mighty muscles into first gear.

It did the trick. In a minute or so afterwards, the shaking stopped completely. And the Millennium Library was still standing. As were we.

*

After Anna had morphed back into her human form, we reconvened on the ground to assess what had caused the damage.

"Could've been an earthquake," Quinn suggested.

"Not in *Winnipeg*!" I said, shocked at the very idea. "That *never* happens here!"

"Yeah," Gerda echoed. "Manitoba's not on a fault line. Thankfully. Otherwise Olivia and I would have a lot more work to do than we do now."

"It could have been a frack," Candas suggested.

"What are you talking about?" asked Anna.

"Oh, come on!" Candas said. "You girls know what a frack is, don't you?"

"Aren't we trying to avoid getting fracked?" Manon asked. "I t'ought you didn't get that happened to ya 'til ya tied the knot!"

"You don't understand," Candace retorted. "I'm talking about hydraulic fracturing!"

"*Fracking*!" I said, understanding what she meant.

"Exactly," answered Candas. "Somebody might have been it doing just outside of town here, and the vibrations from it caused the building to shake. That happens all the time in Alberta."

"How does that work?" Anna asked. "Aren't you supposed to drill for oil deep in the ground?"

"That's the old fashioned Texas way, Anna," said Gerda. "Now, they're more aware of the damage that that method causes to the environment. So they cut small holes with their drills and not gaping maws like they used to."

"The trouble is," Candas explained, "when they suck oil out of the ground that way, they take water out of the ground, too. And you need water in the soil for crops to grow. So they put the water they take out back later, in a different place. That disturbs the equilibrium of the tectonic plates beneath the Earth, and they need to adjust to the change. Hence, earthquakes happen.

And, considering how common fracking is now, earthquakes happen more often, too. Unfortunately for me in particular."

"*HEY!*"

That sharp and unexpected bellow made us turn around in the direction of who had uttered it. Because none of us had.

When we did, we saw a girl around the same age as us, with short, bobbed black hair, and wearing a rugby shirt, sweat pants and heavy workman's boots, standing on one of the concrete ledges at a nearby corner of the park.

"You're *all wrong*, GENIUSES!" she snarled. "*I did* that! All by my lonesome! And I'll do it just as bad to *any* of you *jerks* if ya come anywhere *near* me. Just *try* me if ya don't *believe* me!"

The others were a bit stunned to see this unknown interloper insult them in such a fashion.

Not me.

I knew who this girl was. All too well. You might say that I brought her into the world, and onto myself. She used my method and Lightsound's benevolence to turn herself into the exact opposite of what he and I wanted to do.

And made herself into my most despised enemy. By FAR!

I thought I had gotten rid of her for good the last time we clashed. Evidently, she found a way to escape the metal prison in which I had created for her, in which I threw her half way around the world into the nearest ocean. But she was now here, alive and well.

How was that even possible?

What was even worse was that she was stronger than me. and faster. She had demonstrated that to me with her fists and feet during our fights. Even her muscles were bigger and more formidable looking than mine. She was the "After" picture in a body building ad, and I was merely the "Before".

However, that did not, by any means, stop me from turning purple with rage when I saw her. Nor bellowing out her name with Biblical wrath. To the shock and surprise of my new colleagues, most of whom, by our brief acquaintance, had not thought me capable of such things.

"*GRIDIRON GIRL!*" I roared.

"Hey, Fan-Tan!" she sneered contemptuously at me, using the nickname she coined for me that I loathed. "Long time, no see."

"You abominable piece of TRASH!" I raged. "How DARE you show your face here again! After what you did to me, I ought to…"

"What, exactly, did she do to you for you to hate her like that?" Gerda asked. "Not that it's any of my business…"

"No," I said, turning my back on the villainess and facing them all. "You need to know. She's right- she did it. She's even stronger than I am. Maybe even as strong as you, Gerda. Or all of us together. I don't know. But she can definitely do those kinds of things. I've seen her do worse.

"I told you about all the public speaking stuff I did to promote Tune-Ism, right? Well, at one of them, I got buttonholed by a girl that looked suspiciously like that one does now. Her name was Jacky Hart, and she dug pro football the same way I did superhero cartoons. She asked me, all off-hand and casual like, about whether or not the plan could work if you wanted to be something that existed in the world and wasn't dependent on replicating fantastic illusions. I said, "Sure. Anything's possible if you put your mind to it like I showed you." The next thing I knew…"

"I handed her ass to her," Gridiron Girl cracked. "Some HERO, huh?"

"SHUT UP, YOU!" I ordered, turning around and glaring at her.

"MAKE me!" GG shot back. Then she took off like a bullet from a gun.

"*COME BACK HERE*!" I snarled.

And I took off after her before any of the girls could say or do anything to dissuade me. Even if they wanted to, or if I even wanted to listen to them.

Because I was like a hound on the trail of a fox. I wouldn't stop until I trapped and killed her.

GG had a slight head start. But I was mad. When you're really mad at something or somebody, the distance between you and them is nothing. And I closed the gap quickly.

She had disrespected me, and I wanted revenge. That motivates you to move fast if anything does.

I took a page out of her playbook and tackled her with a ferocious back-pull that would have made Dick Butkus proud of me. It took her legs out from under her, like I wanted. Then I flipped her over so that she could face me. She snarled wordlessly at me, and I snarled wordlessly back, like we were two dogs about to try to kill each other. We wrestled on the ground right then and there.

I knew I didn't stand a chance against her if she prolonged things, so I knew I had to act suddenly before she could use all of her cataclysmic strength against me. After a minute or so of scrapping, I got her up vertically against a concrete wall and fastened a grip as tight as handcuffs on her wrists. And stared into her eyes to convince her that I meant what I said I wanted to do to her.

"Pretty good, Fan-Tan," she taunted me. "You've been working out since last time. But that won't stop the fact that you're still a WIMP!"

"Give me one good reason," I said, blind with hate and rage, "why I shouldn't pull out all your hair with my bare hands, tear that blasphemous tongue out of your mouth, blind your pathetic eyes, rip your second rate casual clothes, and break that Frankenstein monster neck of yours. And *then* throw your dead body into water so deep it will *never* be found!"

As I could not use physical superiority to tame her, I tried to scare her straight by threatening her with death. It was a long shot, but I couldn't have slept that night knowing I hadn't tried to stop her.

I tried. And I failed.

Once I finished speaking, she broke my hold, throwing my arms off her hands swiftly and violently. Then she advanced, menacingly, towards me. To beat me to death, no doubt. As she had threatened to do violently and profanely when I imprisoned her in the ruins of a football stadium's goal post. And I, having no way to stop her, could only back away from her slowly, only briefly prolonging my punishment.

"Here's my "good reason", PAL!" she snarled, like the animalistic gutter punk she was. "You can't do *any* of those things to me. And both of us *know* it. Your little magic princess muscles ain't *nothing* against the combined strength of the *entire* National Football League!"

Which is exactly how powerful she wanted to be. And Lightsound had granted her that power, after I vouched for Jacky with him on her behalf.

Stupid me!

Some most powerful girl in the universe I was. She was that, not me. Worse, she was the most powerful *bully* in the universe.

"You won't…get away with this," I mumbled impotently. "I…"

"SHADDAP!"

With that word, it began.

She raised her left fist and punched me in my face. So hard that teeth were knocked out, and blood spurted out of my mouth. Then her right fist did the same on the other side of my mouth. To the same effect. Then, while I was on the ropes, she raised one of her heavy-booted feet and kicked me in my groin, before I even had a second to cross my legs for protection. The literal kick had so much of a metaphorical kick that I fell backwards onto the pavement, on my butt. Like in the kind of slow motion montage that happens in the movies and television when someone has it happen to them.

Thank God for my ever-present blue bicycle helmet, which, as a safety gesture, I had requested

Lightsound include in my superhero uniform, to appease my own personal fears and my parents' potential ones if they ever found out about my secret life. If I hadn't been wearing it, my melon would have cracked open, and I wouldn't be here now. I guarantee it. GG can kill you with her power, and she doesn't mind doing it at all.

But it was at that moment that Captain Fantastic- the 1.0 model, anyway- died.

My superhero powers and identity disappeared the moment I fell to the ground with a loud crash, replaced by the vastly inferior ones of Olivia Thrift.

Because, as Lightsound told me, my super-heroic identity, as real as it might be to me and others, was merely an illusion he created out of my desire. Illusions like that can only exist- in this world, anyhow- if you truly believe in the possibility that they can be real.

How could I believe I was the most powerful girl in the universe, and the potential conqueror of every evil thing within it, if I was being manhandled by the greatest force of evil I'd ever fought?

Like I was the scared little girl I'd always been. Not the heroine I had wanted to be, and, briefly, was.

Now, I might never be her again.

Back in my civilian clothes and identity, my fate seemed sealed.

"Let me *go*!" I pleaded, getting down on my knees and begging once I realized what had happened to me, and the magnitude of its importance. "*Please*! I....."

She didn't hear my pleas. Instead, she grabbed one of my now weak arms with her hand.

And broke it.

I screamed loud enough to wake the dead, and started crying. My last resort.

"You SADIST!" I shouted, in the midst of my miserable pain. "You've RUINED me! Captain Fantastic is DEAD! You KILLED her!"

"Right," she grunted. "*And Olivia Thrift's* gonna *join* her in the *afterlife* if she don't shut her crybaby mouth!"

"*What*? You mean you *know* who I really *am*?"

"*Of course* I do, you IDIOT! You told it to me *yourself*. When you gave me your business card after we first met. It was right there. "Captain Fantastic, *also known as Olivia Thrift*." That was totally *stupid* of you to do if you wanted to keep it on the down low. You're a *moron*, Thrift!"

"At least *I'm not* a *GOON* with *no feelings*. Like *you* are!"

I made one more attempt to attack her, futilely. She cut me off by putting both of her meat-hook hands around my neck. To choke me, and put me out of my misery.

While I was completely powerless to stop her from doing it.

And then, just at my darkest moment, I was saved.

*

"Turn around, bright eyes!"

It was Muscle Girl. She had come to save me. Like I always dreamed she could or would if I was ever in trouble.

Gridiron Girl discarded me like a spent toy on the ground, and faced her.

"What do *you* want, blondie?" she snapped, in irritation.

In response, MG flew into swiftly before GG could escape, and gave her a taste of her own medicine.

By snapping one of her arms like a dry twig. But her pride wouldn't let her express her pain as I did.

"*What* the *hell*?" GG shouted. "What did I do to you to....?"

"SHUT UP!" MG responded, in a tone that brooked no further arguments. And she pulled GG's eyes to hers so that the full fury in her face could be made evident if it wasn't already, before dropping her to the ground like a mere pebble.

"Yes, Ma'am," a beaten Gridiron Girl mumbled.

"You may not think it was possible," MG told us. "But, back where I came from, I didn't have it easy. I was a preemie. Born about two months before my due date. I was underweight, and weak as a newborn fawn, when I was actually born. I had to spend the first six months of my life in an incubator. And then, I had to make my way around with a walking stick because my legs weren't strong enough to support me on their own. Therefore, I was an easy target for the most sadistic members of my peer group. Especially the girls. They not only maimed me with vindictive insults and accusations, they beat me up in the most savage ways possible. The boys left me alone, by comparison. They could see right away that I was defenseless. And no way was any good-hearted boy- or even a bad one- going to risk his reputation by beating up a defenseless girl. They, unlike the girls, knew better than that.

"Eventually, though, my family moved to Earth, and my days as a defenseless victim of bullying rapidly came to an end. My body became as strong as my mind already was, and I became what I am today. But I *never* forgot what happened there, by any stretch of the imagination. I still get the odd attack of PTSD just vaguely recalling it. So, when I decided to use my physical and mental abilities to become a superhero, I knew exactly who one of the major targets in my fight against evil was going to be. Bullies! Especially FEMALE ones!"

MG grabbed GG's hair so hard it seemed she was going to yank it out at the roots. But she was just being merciful in raising her to her feet. If only temporarily.

"You, *madam*," she spat contemptuously in the bully's face, "are a *disgrace*! To your entire gender! You don't deserve to call yourself a "girl". Because there's a lot you don't seem to understand about what being a girl actually means. Particularly that, if one of us gets physically strong, it won't do for us to throw our weight around on others like us. And not simply because it's not that rigidly sexist concept of being "lady like". A *really* strong girl isn't afraid of being both *strong* and *tender* when the situations call for it. That means she's adaptable, and can handle anything the world gives her. It particularly means that she can respond to what it is, regardless, by being brave. Not through the *cowardice* that always fuels *bullying*. But why I am telling *you* that? You're not a heroine. Heroines have to be like that because people expect more from us than they do villains like you. *A lot* more. Because you villains don't know how to conduct your affairs honorably and honestly, and you never will.

"Now, *get out of my sight*! And if you ever get back into it, you forfeit your *life*. GOT IT?"

GG nodded. At which point, MG released her, turned her around, and kicked her violently in the ass. GG's body flew from the force of the kick over the skyline of Winnipeg and across the Red River, into the farthest regions of St. Boniface, where she presumably fell back to Earth.

She then attended to me. She flew down and sat down beside me, in friendship. Which was what I most needed then.

She didn't ask me if I was hurt. That was redundant. I was- inside and out.

"Where'd she get you?" was what she did say.

"My arm," I groaned. "She broke it, I'm sure. I heard and felt a crack. She broke it like a wishbone."

"Why would you do something that *foolish*, Olivia?"

"What are you talking about, Gerda?"

"You can't fight a super-villain in your civilian identity. That's suicide. Or it would have been for you if I hadn't got here in time."

"I'm not that stupid, Gerda. I fought her as Captain Fantastic. *And then I lost the ability to become her*. She took advantage of me and pounced."

"Lost the ability to....?" Even her mighty Muscle Girl brain seemed to have difficulty grasping that. "Aren't you and she....the same person?"

"No. It's just like how you're a different person entirely when you're Muscle Girl instead of Gerda Munsinger. Only, instead of doing it just with a change of clothes and attitude, I did it by being to cue up the mental image I had of myself as a heroine to become that heroine here in the real world. Don't you remember how I told you Tune-Ism works only if you have enough faith in the reality of the identity of your dreams to make them a reality?"

"Right," she said, on target again. "Like that Monty Python sketch about the apartment building that only stays upright if people believe it's real and not a dream. Otherwise…."

"That's about the size of it," I concurred. "I've lost my faith in my dream, and myself, Gerda. When Gridiron showed up. How could this have happened? I imprisoned her in a Gordian knot I thought she'd never get out of, and she still comes back to *haunt* me!"

"Unfortunately, that's what villains do," she said. "You think you've seen the last of them this time, and they come back. But our lives and jobs would be a bit more boring if they weren't there."

"That's obvious. But what gets my goat is that I got tricked into losing my powers through being goaded into a fight I couldn't possibly win. I was so blind with anger that I couldn't see that until Gridiron socked me in the jaw. Now I'm just like Samson after Delilah got through with him. Weak, helpless and *useless*!"

As I started crying, she held me to my feet, carefully avoiding my broken arm.

"You forgot something," she said, kindly. "Samson got his revenge in the end. At the temple. He got his faith and confidence back when he lost it after his haircut. He stuck it out through his imprisonment, and got through it, and then God gave him back his strength so that he could get vengeance on those who hurt him. There's absolutely no reason why you can't, too. Wallowing in misery when you get slapped down once doesn't solve anything. Trust me- I know."

"I doubt I can do that enough to become Captain Fantastic again. My life and my dreams have been completely shattered."

"Don't be so sure of that. It happens to everyone in this game. You strut around thinking you're hot stuff long enough, and some creature from another world who feeds off physical and mental power eats you for dinner when you're not prepared. I've been through it myself. You remember what happened when that snide little minx Cinnamon Carractacus tricked me into going girl-o a girl-o with her? By threatening to kill my best friend if I didn't?"

"Yeah. She made herself invincible by feeding on your power. Just by grabbing onto your body with her hands. And she made herself strong enough to manhandle and nearly kill you."

"That's true. Fortunately, Bob was able to escape from CC on his own after that, since she let him live. And he found my unconscious body in a river after CC wasted me, and just before I went over a waterfall that might have killed me. I was about to give up, like I did when Petra smacked me down that first time. But Bob wasn't about to even let me try to do that. He really tongue-lashed me for being sorry for myself not having big muscles anymore. He reminded me of all the mental and personal assets that I still had. He had kept track of everything I could do better than I had myself, since he was able to view my adventures in a much more objective way than I ever could. If he hadn't reminded me of how super I was to him, even in a reduced capacity, I might have gone back to that river and drowned in it. 'Cause that was how sad I felt.

"Obviously, that's not what happened. Bob helped me devise a way to trap CC without me having to punch or wrestle or touch her at all, because she would have killed me if she stole what was left of my strength in another fight. That's for sure. But, instead, she fell down and died, and when she did, I got all of my old mojo back.

"So, like I said, it happens to everyone. The good thing is, you get over it real quick, and then you can get back to business. Once you get confident enough to get Captain Fantastic back to life, it'll be just the same for you. What you can't do is let it knock you out forever. That's the coward's way out. And you know how I feel about cowards."

"I think I can do all of that. Maybe once this arm heals, it'll be easier for the rest of me to heal, too."

"That's the spirit. Think about it like this: it's how you look at everything. It can be honey- that is, good tasting. Like the gratitude people give you for rescuing you or saving the world or what not. It helps you feel good, and makes you glad you can do stuff other people can't if they react like that. But it can also be salt- bitter and hard to swallow on its own, but important in preserving and keeping you fresh, and making it clear to you why your job matters and why you still need to do it. The villains in particular, for obvious reasons. But also all of those stupid cretins and morons, especially of the adult variety, who let their basic animal passions for power and money permanently interfere with their ability to see what's good for everybody and not just themselves. They're more dangerous to our existence than any villain could be, as hard as that might be to believe, because you can't get rid of them as easily as you can your common garden-variety villain. Even super powers are no match for bureaucracy and Machiavellian politics sometimes. But you'll find that out on your own soon enough.

"Point is, either too much honey or too much salt is bad for you. Like anything else...."

She might have continued her discourse for a while, because sometimes she doesn't know when to stop when she gets going like that. Still, I would have lapped up any sort of advice she could have given me. Anything to be half the heroine she was.

But she was interrupted, fatefully, by some horrific screaming. From back at the Library, which wasn't too far away.

Chapter Five: The League

The screaming was coming from the direction where we had come. The Consortium had obviously gotten into trouble since we left them hanging.

"Hurry!" MG said, gripping the hand attached to my good arm with her unbreakable grip. "No time to lose!"

I held on for dear life for the short duration of the flight, and hoped we could still arrive in time.

We couldn't. We were too late to do anything.

They were all gone.

All trace of them had vanished. There was no indication that the gals had put up any kind of struggle or fight whatsoever, although undoubtedly they must have given it the old college try. It almost seemed like they had never been there to begin with.

The only evidence of what had happened was a small piece of paper tucked into one of the concrete mounds surrounding the park. MG found it, quickly read it, and then crumpled it forcefully in her mighty fist. Before throwing it in the nearest recycling bin, that is.

"Well," she said, ruefully and sarcastically. "This is just what we need!"

"Who did it?" I asked.

"The Merch!" she pronounced.

I gasped, in horror.

"We have your nemesis to thank for it," she said. "They cooked up that whole thing as a ruse to trap us after they found her in that trap of yours- and freed her from it. They paid her handsomely- of course- to taunt all of us, not just you, and get us to move in striking distance of their abduction ray. Which was how the rest of them got nabbed. Your decision to run after her, and mine to back you up- because you obviously needed it- threw a wrench into their plans.

"That's the only good thing about this. Because the Merch have got them trapped now. Along with the other people and things they steal from other planets. Up in that elephantine spaceship of theirs."

"What's going to happen to them?"

"Nothing good. They'll be held in captivity, under the most sophisticated means available. In some specially created and assigned cells, like animals in a pound or pet shop. They stay there until some well-heeled alien takes a fancy to one of them- because, at *their* prices, that's all they can *afford* - and makes them his or her servant - for *life*. No - not servant. *Slave*. That's more accurate. The other option is they stay in there until when and if they die. Whichever comes first."

"But surely they can use their powers to...."

"They know all their weaknesses. Physical, mental and psychological. They know those of most of the supes in the universe. That's how they keep us under control in captivity. Easier for keeping a super-powered slave under control than any cat o' nine tails."

"How is that possible?"

"They have a network of paid informants and sources a mile long. Including most of the super-powered bad guys and gals in the universe who work freelance, and need the money to finance their nasty schemes against us. That goes for your acquaintance, and all of mine. It's another of their bargaining chips against us. They think it'll scare us into silence. It doesn't, and it never will. We don't scare that easy by any means."

"So they know your weakness?"

"Yes," she said.

As Gerda, and not Muscle Girl. Very soft, not loud, like she normally did as a hero. For she could not be completely fearless admitting that. It took her nearly a minute to say it, when she's usually very prompt and confident in her replies. But I knew exactly how she felt. I felt the same myself. Entirely.

"Would they have known Captain Fantastic's? I mean, if I hadn't short-circuited myself back there…"

"That,"- she was MG again, and confident- "is the only silver lining in all of this. You're still new by their standards. Generally, they don't start tracking you unless you have at least a year's…"

I interrupted her by bursting into tears, and she embraced me.

"*This is all my fault*!" I wailed.

"NO!" she said in her firmest tone. So I stopped crying and listened to her speak again.

"We still would have been caught and captured. Regardless. That was their plan. Goad one or all of us into blatant anger that would get the better of our reason, and then strike before we could do even the remotest damage to them or their agents. Any of us would have reacted the same if our most hated foe showed up unexpectedly here and cut us like that. If Petra had been there, I would have reacted the same. But they know who you are, anyway, even if they aren't tracking you. Why would they have sent your enemy to do it and not one of mine or the others' if that wasn't the case?

"Maybe I should have had the girls come with me instead of telling them to stay put. Then things might have been different. But we can't do anything about that now. No use crying over spilled milk, so to speak."

"Is there anything you can do to stop them?"

"There *is* something we can *do*."

"So you don't think badly of me for....?"

"You need to stop blaming yourself for these things when they happen to you," she remonstrated. "You know as well as anybody you can't do anything when you're just a pawn in someone else's game. That's how the Merch may roll, but it doesn't mean we have to sink to their level.

"To elaborate on my answer to your first question, there is something we can do. Though not the two of us alone. This isn't the kind of thing Muscle Girl can handle on her own, nor is the kind of thing that Captain Fantastic would be able to, either, if she were still alive and kicking. *This* is a job for the International League of Girls with Guns!"

"It's that bad, huh?"

"*That* bad, indeed. The only way the Merch can be possibly be destroyed, or even temporarily crippled, is for us to have all the firepower we can get. The kind of thing you can only do when you're with the only people in the universe who know how you feel, how you think and how you act just as good as you do. If not better. I'm very fortunate to have lucked into that kind of situation. *Very*. And maybe, when you get all better, you will, too, if you end up as fortunate as I've been."

Once again, as when she proffered her friendship, I completely screamed with joy inside. Not just a chance to meet and befriend her, but possibly *all* of my idols *at once*!

"Would I actually get to meet them all? I mean, if there's time for...."

"Sure. If you want, I mean."

"Are you *kidding*? I do! Why would you think for a moment I *wouldn't*? That's the *other* dream of mine that I thought would never come true! That I'd actually meet all of you, and you'd treat me like a peer. Instead of some crazy, delusional so-called "fan". Like *way* too many of those so-called "fans" of you actually are. Not the true believers like me, of course. The phonies, and the sycophants. The ones who only want you for what they can get out of you, and don't give you anything back in return."

"No need to tell me about any of *those* folks," MG interjected, rolling her eyes.

"Even if I can't help you as Captain Fantastic," I continued, "I can certainly help you as Olivia Thrift. I owe it to the Consortium to help free them. And to you, for genuinely befriending me. When you *easily* could have put on airs and given me the coldest of shoulders.

We need to get them out, if only so that their enemies can step in and take over in their absence. Because that's what happens when a hero goes down. If the heroes aren't doing their jobs, the villains win. By default. No contest!"

"Again, you're preaching to the choir."

"Besides, my Mom can't come here and pick me up until 6- even if I *wanted* to go home. She works until then. And Dad's back in Headingley on duty at the jail, and he can't just...."

"No need to explain that. My parents are working stiffs, too. Soldiers back in the old home land, and corporate scientists in the here and now. Long hours, and not enough time for you always. The advantage - and the *disadvantage* - of that is you get much more of a chance to grow up on your own terms, and become your own person. The kind that even they can't tell you what to do if you don't let them. We're both like that, Olivia. The gals in the Consortium are the same, as are the girls in the League. That's why we all click when we're together. We all believe in the same things, and work towards the same goals. We use different means, and different methods, and disagree about what works best when a lot, I know. But the important things is we all want the same objective, and can work towards it together without breaking down and hating on each other permanently. That's what our enemies do all the time, and it completely undoes them. Always."

She started pawing herself frantically.

"Rats!"

"What?"

"I left my cell phone in the john when I changed. With my civvies. I'll have to…"

"You could just use mine, instead."

I gave it to her after I took it out of the pocket of my dress.

"This may not come cheap for you, given the highway robbery rates they charge where my pals all live," she warned me. "Won't your parents be upset if it costs a lot? They're paying for it, aren't they?"

"No. I pay my own bill. With whatever I can scrape up, since I don't have a job yet. They told me that was the cost of having a phone. Along with not wasting too much time in pointless gabbing on it. So I got to ration when I use it. I'm okay with that. It's part of being the conscientious and responsible person I want to be. But this is more than worth it. Especially after today, I know all about sacrifices."

So she went off, and started contacting the League.

*

It didn't take long for them to come.

Muscle Girl only called one of them, it seemed, and the others found out about it through their internal grapevine. That was all it took. Those five ladies must have some kind of second sight or ESP when it comes to each other. That would explain why they work so well as a team. Though probably not why they fight with each other so much over stupid things.

In any event, each of them made a triumphant entrance into Winnipeg from an entirely different geographic direction. I felt like a kid in a candy store watching them come in.

The Brat came from the North, right from outer space. Breaking the sound barrier as she did, which is what all of them can do when they fly, and displaying her unstoppable courage on her face completely. Her blonde-haired toddler's appearance, and the clothing related to it- blue sweater open to reveal a white T shirt with a giant "B" on it, white skirt and boots-was as effective as disguising her true abilities as Gerda's civilian identity. And both of them delighted in defanging anyone who was deluded enough to think of them as a "mere" or "helpless" girl. Especially in the Brat's case, because, unlike Gerda, she was actually an *adult* alien.

Then Power Bunny came up from the South, from business in the United States. The light blue shirt and skirt she wore contrasted sharply with the feminine pink tones of her fur. Cheerful optimism, and her trademark humor, seemed to pour out of her, given the broad grin she had on her face. But that was a given, considering she was a denizen of the marvelous realm of Anthropomorph, where all of the creatures known pejoratively as "cartoon characters", whom we see in the movies and television as mere 2D and 3D images, are living, breathing, full dimensional beings like humans are here. So the physical limitations of our universe mean nothing to her, and she can use the unique abilities of her race to their full advantage here. Although she also has more traditional super powers, thanks to an encounter with a runaway meteorite doing her day job as a journalist, to go along with them as backup. Making her even more formidable than the ones of her kind who don't have that in their arsenal.

Cerberus was next, coming out from the West. She was and is a magnificent specimen of canine womanhood, despite being in the permanent physical position of being a big-eared, big-eyed and runty looking Dalmatian puppy. She was the product of a union between a normal Earth dog and a member of an alien, superpower laden species of same, the Perros, based around Sirius, the Dog Star. So, as she puts it, she got her dad's powers and her mom's good looks in one bargain. Once again, a very deceptive looking package able to pack a punch at the right moments. As she flew in, with a series of lusty yips and an earth-shaking howl, it seemed I could see every single black spot on her white fur coat gleam. Even the ones her monogrammed white T actually obscured.

Finally, from the East, came Candy Girl, the Titan of Teens herself. A red-haired, black-eyed goddess in appearance, as tall as a WNBA or women's college basketball player, with the muscles, the speed and the moves to match. She managed to look drop dead gorgeous despite her largely utilitarian uniform of purple monogrammed sweatshirt, purple sweatpants, red belt and yellow work boots. Her emerald ring, the source of all of her mighty powers, gleamed like a beacon from the ring finger of her right hand. It had been given to her by a boy named Cantus, actually an intergalactic policeman-type of some note, after she had rescued him from drowning while on duty as a lifeguard. After he tragically died soon afterwards, he bequeathed the ring and all the responsibilities related to it to her. And, as he was the first one she truly loved- and possibly the only one, by her own estimation- she was not in any sort of position to refuse. It took her some time to discover the magnitude of her position, though, especially when many of Cantus' old enemies started gunning for her instead. But she's managed to very good at her job, in spite of, among other things, her short temper. Having a younger brother with genius-level intelligence to confide in at difficult times helps as well. And she has to confide in him more than you think. Her brain is afflicted with Asperger's syndrome, that particular subgroup of Autism that makes those with it frequently zig when others think they should zag. This comes about frequently in the person of her sudden and unexpected losses of confidence in herself and her abilities, which can often come at the worst of possible times. But her triumphs over her enemies are far sweeter for this reason alone than they would be otherwise.

Alas, Candy- who is more likely than the others, for some reason, to have the wind taken out of her sails unexpectedly, and for seemingly and entirely capricious reasons- was humiliated coming down out of the air as they were not. A sudden and unexpected gust of wind blew her off course from her intended landing place- along with the others near MG and me- and directly towards the reflecting pool of water around most of Millennium Library Park. Where she landed with a yell- and an undignified splash.

Needless to say, she wasn't pleased.

That was made clear by the first words I heard any of them utter in my presence.

In a sandpaper-rough tone completely and unexpectedly at odds with her angelic physical appearance, Candy swore profusely in the most unprintable language imaginable.

She furiously climbed out of the pool and joined the rest of us nearby, shaking with rage. Her uniform, unlike her friends', was not as indestructible as her body. It certainly wasn't waterproof.

"Who, in their right mind, thought THAT was a good idea?" she snapped, gesturing to the pool with her hands. "HUH? Who puts a POOL right in a decent superhero's *flight path*? I got my *dignity* to consider when I make my entrances! Just as much as you lucky slobs do! Don't the morons who pull the purse strings around here know the first thing about making our job EASY to do instead of *HARD*?"

"Cut the noise, Candy!" said Power Bunny, with more than a bit of annoyance, as she gestured to the building behind us. "Don't you know that this place is a library? You might be forcing somebody to curtail their literacy activities in there."

"Yeah," the Brat added, in deeper tones than her youthful body seemed capable of producing. "*Keep* that up and some old lady librarian will be out here in a second, telling us that our music's too loud."

"We are not in the *library* itself," Candy retorted. "The rules *inside* there don't apply out *here*. And I am NOT making *NOISE*!!"

"I, for one, would disagree with that," Muscle Girl interjected. "As would, perhaps, the entire city of Winnipeg."

She icily turned the full force of her glare onto Candy, who succumbed into placid silence after mumbling an apology under her breath.

"Besides which," she continued, "we have *more* serious things to consider right now than *merely* whether we got our panties soaked in water or not, as you all know by now. But first, an introduction is in order." She turned in my direction and gestured. "Ladies, this is my currently beleaguered Canadian comrade-in-arms, Olivia Thrift. Whom some of you may know as the best friend and confidant of..."

"*Cap*-tain *Fan*-tas-tic!"

Those were Cerberus' first words, spoken in that beguiling, enchanting and hypnotic voice, and unique grammatical and phonetic cadences, that are hers and hers alone. She stared at me with her gigantic eyes, looking at me like she was a snake and I was her next meal. But there was no malice in her manner at all. I knew, as we all did, that she was a good-natured, New Age intellectual at heart, but not unafraid to flex her formidable physical and mental muscles at any time required. Particularly in the presence of her equally formidable enemies, of which, thankfully, I was not one. Far from it! We clearly admired each other, based on what we knew of each other (or, at the very least, her knowledge of Captain Fantastic's preceded reputation), and that made it so much easier for me to return her admiring stare with one of my own. As it did for me to feel the astonishingly large reserve of Herculean power that seem to course through her Lilliputian body, when she put one of her forepaws in my hand to signify how friendly she truly was.

"She," she said to me, "is a *treasure*! She does EXACTLY what all of us wish we could do if we didn't have this save-the-world *schtick* as our personal albatrosses. My personal philosophy is that there is nothing that is more important for an ethical super-heroine to have - nothing *whatsoever*- than a) always having good PR with the outside world, and b) *possibly* inspiring a younger generation of would-be heroes of another generation to follow in her footsteps. The same way the Pied Piper emptied Hamelin entirely of people like you a long time ago. She has *both* of those things. In *spades*. Some of us are lucky to have the first one, but the second one is a real diamond in the rough. And yet *somehow* she managed to do *both* of them, and give all of us in the superhero business a five-alarm wake-up call that, in spite of all our success combatting evil, we aren't as all that as we sometimes think. I mean, "Tune-Ism" alone is a *godsend*! I know something about having a strong mind, and how to use its secrets, but it never even *occurred* to me that there was the chance to achieve everything you wanted simply by looking at it on the all-mighty cathode ray and saying, "Let it be done." Hot diggity dog ziggity *boom*! She's like Wonder Woman and Dale Carnegie in the same BODY! All I can say to that is, "Bra-*vo*!"

After such a ringing endorsement, I suddenly felt as if I was in a cartoon, after being crushed unexpectedly by a boulder. I was going to have to do the same thing to Cerberus by telling her about CF's unpleasant demise. I dreaded that, greatly.

Fortunately, MG deflected this from me by telling Cerberus a slight fib when she asked it would be possible to actually meet the fellow heroine who had impressed her so much.

"Unfortunately, CF is MIA right now, Cerb'," she said.

"*What*?" Cerberus was outraged. "How did it happen?"

"The Merch got her," MG responded, smoothly. "Along with nearly all of the Canadian Consortium. Just like that."

Everyone was silent for a moment, as they pondered the implications.

"They're a thorough bunch, aren't they?" the Brat said to break the lull. "I'll give them that much, at least."

"You have to be if you're *them*, Brat," PB interjected. "People who worship the Almighty Dollar always are. That way, they can get not just somebody, but *everybody*."

"True," added Cerberus. "Although the Almighty Dollar's not going to cut it in this case. Dollars, after all, aren't in circulation much except here in Canada and in the United States, and some odd place on Earth here and there, like Australia. The Merch's clients aren't human beings from Earth but aliens from outer space. So we're dealing more with the Almighty Credit here."

"It's not the currency that matters," said Candy. "It's what you decide to *do* with it."

"Exactly, Candy," responded Cerberus. "Worshipping money, in any shape or form, is worse than doing it with any other Golden Calf."

"It's only a means to an end," said MG. "Whether you're rich *or* poor."

"Well, what are we standing around here for?" Candy said. "We need to go up there and throw those moneychangers out of our temple."

"And so we shall," said a determined Cerberus.

She turned to me.

"Olivia, as you are flightless, you will require one of us to transport you there and back, no doubt. So I volunteer."

"I couldn't impose on you like that," I said, modestly.

"You're not imposing, because I don't mind at all. And it's important you come, because you'd be able to help us out in a pinch if everything goes Pete Tong.

Every basketball team needs a sixth man to come in if one of the others busts his leg playing. That's why we usually have at least one of our mortal pals along for the ride. If they're not the ones being kidnapped or victimized themselves, that is."

"I'm just worried about you being able to support my weight. I might crush you if…."

Cerberus gave me a look that said *shut up, you idiot* better than she could have said herself, which is hard to do. That only lasted a second, for she smiled, knowingly and broadly, after that, before resuming speaking.

"I'm surprised that such a diligent scholar of our craft- as MG has told all of us you very much are, and we *appreciate* that, by the way- would even *momentarily* forget who we are and what we are capable of doing merely based on external appearance. I consider excessive bragging immodest, but I am *not* bragging when I say that I am *more* than capable of supporting a slip of a girl like you on my back. I mean, you've seen yourself what I can do with just my TAIL, haven't you?

"I say that because you do not, as you seem to assume, have to ride me like a common horse. All you need to do is hold onto my aforementioned tail, and you are just peachy. Only do *not* let go. For *any* reason. Because I might not be able to catch you if you fall, and they might not, either.

"That is, unless one of the other ladies wants to relieve me of the responsibility of transporting you."

They did not. And so, with me hanging on to Cerberus' tail as tight as I could, we sailed off into outer space.

Chapter Six: The Shop

It didn't take us long to get out where we needed to be. Even though I and the others were going at FTL speed, and I was then a mere mortal compared to them, I wasn't adversely affected. Cerberus really meant it when she spoke of her tail. It was as powerful as the rest of her body put together, even when like I held onto it like a brass ring on a carousel. She never once complained. Or even noticed I was there, since she never turned around to look at me.

But it helped that I no longer had super strength, I suppose. Not nearly as much pressure exerted.

On the way, as they spoke to each other and me, I learned what I needed to know about the Merch that I didn't already.

They weren't a "race" of people, in the biological sense of that term, but rather an intergalactic social, political and economic men's club, with members from all across the universe. All of which were either Caucasian by birth or could easily pass as such here. Other minorities, particularly women of all races and men of some, were not allowed. They were particularly hard on younger girls like us, for they believed erroneously we were largely inferior physically to men. Based only on the fact that women of all races and species tend to be shorter and weigh less than men physically, and also due to that business in the Bible about Eve simply being an evolved form of one of Adam's ribs. Though this discounts the variances in genetics and evolution that allow for girls who are taller than many men (like Candy) or smarter than many of them (like Muscle Girl and Cerberus).

There was also that peculiarly female malady, hysteria, leading to insanity, to consider. The Brat, Candy, and PB are the only ones who have had periods yet (Cerberus, though an adult in mindset, has a body that will never "grow up"), and they testified to how even they didn't trust themselves during their "times" of the month, which were worsened by their super powers rather than made better. All of us have gotten like that at one time. Candy and PB have each gone stark raving bonkers, and they thought that was even worse than their periods.

Undoubtedly, the Merch members were on the business end of angry women and girls at many times in their lives, and they coalesced these experiences into a misogynistic stereotype that is only partially true. Because that's what they were- misogynists. If you have had a bad experience with something, it colors your experience of it in a negative light. And more than one bad experience convinces you that your victimizer is not like you at all. Different. And therefore, must be suppressed so that your way of thinking can be proved correct and that of the other wrong.

If the League could be believed, the Merch was only interested in women if they blatantly offered their bodies to them, either for money or not, or if it was possible to keep them in the style the Merch wanted them kept in. In their "proper" place. And, if they did not, there was a whole constellation of physical and psychological things they could get girls and women to do to the men or each other. In order to get them to "behave", and do what "Papa" liked.

The League was really taking a risk in doing this. The Merch could eviscerate them from the face of the Earth with all the resources they had. To say nothing of what they could do to defenseless Olivia Thrift if they caught her.

The Merch hated girls and women with super powers, or did heroic deeds, even more than the normal kind. They were all female creatures who were "better" than them at pretty much everything, and thus a blatant and enormous threat to their masculine pride. So that was why it was these ones- and not the men, whom they supposedly might be able to talk or fight with on the save level- they targeted when they wanted to expand their "collection" from things from Earth. Knocking them out and capturing them and such was a political statement of apocalyptic consequences to feminists of all sectional persuasions.

And the League was the biggest exception to the Merch's conception of the world possible. Five girls of different ages and species, harmoniously (for the most part) employing tactics together and apart that hit the Merch where it hurt. What's not to hate?

This would be the first time, however, that the League entered Merch territory instead of vice versa, so all bets on us coming out all alive were off. They had faced agents of them elsewhere in the universe before on their own, and defeated them easily, like always. But coming there as a group made them vulnerable to being captured and destroyed as a group as well.

Another group of heroines- the Consortium- had just gone through this humiliating process. And the

League was as determined to free and avenge them as I was.

Yet we had to do so by avoiding the greatest threat the Merch posed to us. It wasn't physical, but psychological. Instead of making them dance to our tune with a few roundhouse punches and kicks, they could make us dance to theirs by dangling ridiculous, superficial and irrelevant promises in front of us- the complete opposite of what I promised to do for kids with Tune-Ism- by persuading us they were good deep in our minds. They used deception, con artistry, visual and aural illusions, and hard-sell advertising nearly as effectively against the wills and desires of their victims as the League employed its own super powers. They warned me, in particular, considering I did not have the kind of super will power they had, not to succumb to any sort of temptation the Merch might dangle in front of me. Otherwise, I might become a prisoner of their glamour. *Forever.*

That, however, would be something that would be tested in all of us, and soon.

*

The Merch ship was much larger than I could have imagined. It almost seemed as if the Empire from *Star Wars* had just had a military surplus sale, and the Merch had scooped up a lot of their extra gear on the cheap. It was natural, though, that the ship was the same color as a slab of vanilla ice cream. Our multi-colored clothing, fur, hair and eyes caused us to become a somewhat garish-looking *bas relief* against the white walls, cavernous hallways and seemingly endless floors.

Alas, we weren't able to complete escape our enemies' prying eyes with stealth, as we had planned. For we were quickly surrounded by what was the Merch's first line of defense, a group of ghoulish-looking androids so frightening-looking that they made me scream when they surprised us.

"GET DOWN!" MG shouted at me.

She didn't mean dance to a funky beat.

So I immediately tried to make myself as inconspicuous as I possibly could, as the League fought a vicious tooth-and-nail scrap with the androids from my vantage point. Horrible sounds of grunts, groans, punches, kicks, tackles, profanity, barking, mental illusions and projections, lifts and tosses, lasers and other weaponry fired, bodies slammed against walls and floors, and the odd yell or yelp of surprise filled the air. I covered my eyes through the affair and saw none of it, though I heard it all.

The struggle seemed endless, for the might and the metaphysical abilities of the androids almost seemed to be equal to those of the League, and came close to defeating them. But, ultimately, the combined strength, speed, agility and intelligence of the League led them to victory, as was usually the case in these scenarios. Soon, what was left of the androids was merely garbage on the floor, and I was able to emerge from the place where I had sequestered myself, unharmed.

I rejoined my mighty idols, who, while physically unharmed, had been mentally wounded by the sudden and entirely unexpected ambush.

"This is going to be tougher than I thought," said Cerberus, for once no longer completely sure of herself and her abilities. "I had *no* idea that they would have such sophisticated security protocols in place. No idea *whatsoever*. Why, they nearly finished us off!"

"The key word is 'nearly', Cerb'," said PB. "We finished *them* off, instead!"

"We sure did," said the Brat. "Because it's obvious the Merch want us *alive*, and not dead. If it were the other way, they'd have pumped us full of our Achilles by now and left us to rot."

"Don't *say* that, Brat!" Candy interjected, with a sudden panicked sob in her voice. "Just…DON'T! You gals bring up weaknesses, and I start thinking about all of *mine*. And I won't *STOP*!" She started crying hysterically. "I'm no good to you in that condition. I….."

"*Stop it*!" Muscle Girl snapped, in a chastising tone. "This is *no time* for PSYCHOANALYSIS!"

The words- and one eye- were directed at Candy, who quickly sobered up. The other eye glared sharply at the Brat, for bringing up the usually verboten topic of their singular and joint weaknesses so bluntly in public. She sobered up, too.

"Sorry," she mumbled apologetically.

"Save the *drama* for your *mamas*, girls," Cerberus said. "We got to *save* somebody. And we *WILL*!"

So saying, she smashed through one of the walls with her speed, and the others followed suit through the hole she created. As did I, much more slowly and less confidently, moments later.

Being powerless, it took me nearly an hour to make my way through the poorly lit and cavernous ship. My inability to travel with them had unintentionally caused them to discard me easily, though I knew full well none of them would allow me to perish or otherwise get hurt while they had a chance of defending me. And, as I could not find a shopping mall-style key grid to help me understand exactly where I was or where I could go, my progress was limited in the extreme. But my intelligence had not been lost along with the rest of my super powers, and I knew this would be the last resort I could use if I was to get caught.

Then, suddenly, I was reunited with Muscle Girl and Cerberus when they re-emerged, levitating in the air close above me.

"You haven't seen the others, have you, Olivia?" Cerberus asked.

"No," I said. "I haven't seen them since we were all together last. You don't think they're....dead. Are they?"

"That's nonsense, and you know it," said Muscle Girl. "It takes much more to kill us than normal folks like you. No offense."

"None taken," said I.

"We are, however," interjected Cerberus, "concerned for their current location, and their current state of mind. They seemed to have entered a quagmire on both counts."

"What do you mean?" I asked.

"We think the Merch have got them," MG said. "And *brainwashed* them. They're not as smart as Cerb' and I are, though only in formal IQ measurements. The street smarts they have in spades don't count in those kind of assessments."

"It's just like with the Merch's other victims," Cerberus continued. "They find the stupidest and most gullible people in a group, and get them to believe anything is possible by playing to their desired dreams and not the actualities in their lives. Particularly by managing to match their dreams up with some commercial commodity that most directly and clearly embodies those dreams. As those mad men in the advertising industry have done with our minds for *decades*. Our powers make us able to fight and think and jump and run very well, yes. But we have absolutely no defense against the awesome might of the so-called "art" of *persuasion*. When it is done, it is done. That's what so scary about the Merch. Once they get going on something or somebody, they don't stop until they've got it all. They're greedy, they're insane, and they're more dangerous to our bodies and minds than the rest of our enemies *put together*!"

"Wait a minute," MG said. "Do you hear something?"

"Yeah," I added. "That sounds like the three of them together."

"Sure is," Cerberus agreed. "I'd recognize Candy's air-raid-siren bawl anywhere."

It actually was only around the corner from where we had reconvened, and down the hall. The sound was clearly coming from behind a broker door with no knob. Over what remained of what had been frosted glass, a legend was written in handwriting on a piece of paper:

WHAT YOU WANT IS IN HERE

So, what else could we do? We went inside.

*

The room was set up like some sort of mass market, everything-in-one shop. Something like an intergalactic version of Wal-Mart, or Target. Everything was stacked neatly into aisles, with placards hanging from the ceiling numbering the aisles, and explaining to the last detail what was in each aisle and where to find it. Along with extremely garish "sale" signs promising astronomical levels of savings on all purchases, and signs saying things like "WE'RE GIVIN' IT TO YA!" and "YOU KNOW YOU *WANT* IT!" around almost every corner. Tinny Muzak was heard on a public address system, both stemming from an unknown source. I half-expected some elderly man in a blue vest to come forward and "welcome" us there, or for some nasal-voiced announcer to interrupt the Muzak to demand a "clean up" in one of the aisles.

The Merch did their homework on their intended victims- before they struck them down like cobras.

"Know how I know this is fake?" Cerberus asked.

"How?" I asked back.

"Because if it were," she explained, "they would throw me out the moment I walked in. Or *try* to."

"Not *this* again," Muscle Girl said, rolling her eyes.

"Is it because you're a dog?" I asked again.

"Don't get her started," MG warned me *sotto voce*. But it was too late.

"And the lady wins a CIGAR!" Cerberus exclaimed. "That, Olivia, is the crux of the issue *exactly*.

True, I may be intelligent, and strong, and fast, and agile. As well as being able to be better to you than you are to yourself with my endless reserves of sympathy and empathy. But I have my LIMITS! And one of them is the many occasions when, in spite of what I can do and say, I am STILL treated in the eyes of *way too many common human beings* as a mere CRETIN! On a *daily basis*, yet….."

"Wow," I whispered to MG, as Cerberus continued to….bitch….in the background. "She's got *issues*. I'm sorry I triggered her like that. I had no idea I was…."

"You do now," MG answered. "She's like a Roman candle. Get her going, and she'll go for as long as she thinks you're listening, but she'll stop as soon as you stop or you tell her to cut the jive. Trust me. I've known her longer than you. Practically anything dumb like that can set her off. She's almost as bad as the Merch can be when it comes to luring you into traps. We're just fortunate she's on *our* side.

"The important thing is, you learned it was wrong, and, because of that, you know to never do it again once you know why and how it happens. That's all I care about. Besides, we're getting close to the source now, so she'll have to…."

She did. And we did, too. Because we were now at ground zero of the current quagmire we faced.

We were in aisle number three, which, according to its placard, sold toys and other products aimed at children.

Which was *exactly* what the Brat, Power Bunny and Candy Girl were acting like!

They were running around like teenagers after the Beatles in the 1960s, screaming and jumping around excitedly with some sort of things in their hands. This was where the Brat's child-like appearance might have gotten her a free pass for acting like such a moron. Candy and PB didn't even have *that* excuse. No teenage girl or young lady rabbit would dare act like that if they had reputations and sanity to consider!

Cerberus brought the immature frolic to an abrupt stop by issuing one of her powerful sonic barks, which can disable even the mightiest eardrums temporarily. Mine rang for several minutes afterwards with the echo. But it got them down on the floor, which was what Cerberus wanted.

We confronted them, scowling, as soon as they got to their feet.

"*What* did you think you were DOING?" Cerberus growled. "This is no time for FRIVOLITIES!"

"You call *this a frivolity*?" Candy retorted, rhetorically.

She produced a comic book, protected by a mylar bag and a couple of layers of thick tape. And on its front cover was.....

The International League of Girls with Guns.

Just as they looked and acted in "real" life.

"#1 Collector's Edition, baby!" Candy crowed. "And dig who wrote it!"

"*NEIL GAIMAN*!" Muscle Girl exclaimed.

She said the man's name as I would have said her own in the presence of others, with wide eyes and hands clasped. As if he were one of the Olympic or Nordic gods he has written about in the past.

It was far too easily done. She was trapped by the Merch without being able to throw a single mighty punch in defense of her honor.

"Darn right," Candy continued. "Those idiots at DC finally figured out where the *real* action is. We *made* it, girls. The BIG TIME!"

"What, exactly, is so good...?" an unconvinced Cerberus began.

"Don't you *get* it, Cerb'?" Power Bunny interrupted, continuing Candy's crowing. "*Nobody* takes you *seriously* as a supe unless you're in at least *one* comic book! That was how it all *began*!"

"And now people will," said an excited Brat. "Take us seriously, I mean. We *got* ours. Together *and* apart. And it won't be just Gaiman writing about us, either. We all got assigned to rock-star writers! I got Brian Michael Bendis, PB got J. Michael Straczynski, and Candy got Kelly Sue DeConnick!"

The three of them failed to suppress obvious and infectious schoolgirl giggles.

"Aw!" Muscle Girl said enviously. "I'm jealous. Don't Cerb' and I rate anyone that good?"

"Leave me *out* of this, you *traitor*!" Cerberus growled, trying and failing to get a rise from MG.

"Don't worry, MG!" Candy gushed. "They got you two covered, too. You, MG, are going to be written about by *Genevieve Valentine*!"

"*A speculative fiction prose writer*!" said Muscle Girl. "I sure am *lucky*!"

"Yep," said the Brat. "But we really envy you, Cerberus."

"Why?" said that worthy.

"Because," said PB, "you are going to be the main attraction in a comic scripted by none other than STAN LEE *himself*!"

"STAN LEE?"

It takes a lot to impress that little girl, and the Merch had pulled out the biggest gun they had in order to do it. She clearly felt the same level of admiration for him MG had for Neil Gaiman, because her reaction to hearing his name was exactly the same as hers!

Well, we *all* like Stan. Most of us wouldn't be who we are today without him. But that's beside the point.

The point was that Cerberus had been ensnared by their swan song. The entire League had been!

"I thought he *stopped* writing a long time ago," Cerberus said. "And that he was a Marvel man forever. Wow. This is the *greatest* honor I *ever* could have received in my LIFE!"

"I have no idea how it happened," Candy explained. "We just turned the corner and BOOM! They've all been written, drawn and printed and made available for sale here. We didn't know a damn thing beforehand! But they obviously know who we are. Otherwise…"

"Won't the *other* comic book heroes mind you cutting in on their action?" I said, trying to restore reality to the discussion.

"They," said Candy, contemptuously, "can go to HELL. Those priggish *jerks* have done absolutely

NOTHING for ANY of us since we got in the game! NOTHING! Even though we're *better* than all of them *put together*! We can do *their* job better than *they* can with their eyes *blindfolded*."

"And why would a place like this sell *comics*, anyhow?" I continued in inquisitive tones, although now much more to myself than to them. "The stuff in these kinds of stores is all on the cheap. You actually get most comic books in actual comic book *stores* nowadays. And many of them are expensive!"

"That's not all," interjected the Brat. "We all got our own *action figures*!" She whipped out a small plastic duplicate of herself with a cord dangling. "And they *talk*!" She pulled the cord, and her doppleganger spewed out a string of incomprehensible gobbledygook in a small, tinny and badly recorded voice.

"And then there's the *DVDs*!" PB added. She sped away quickly, and returned in seconds with a massive brick of plastic under her arm.

"Look at *this*!" she said, holding it up so we could all see it clearly.

It was a case for a DVD compilation of what appeared to be a complete run of a television series from some time ago. But it wasn't. The case had the logo the International League of Girls with Guns used to identify their brand with the public, a gold medallion with *bas reliefs* of the five of them inside. And, as it was with the comics, they burst out of the logo as themselves as they were in real life and nothing else. Beneath that was written, in full bold type, "THE COMPLETE SERIES".

"Can you *believe it*?" she exclaimed. "This is even BETTER than comics! 'Cause everyone knows how immortal CARTOON CHARACTERS can be if they just give us a chance to *live* here on Earth. And I should know! I'm ONE of them! We belong to the ages now! And not just a puny one or two season run, neither. Looks like the *schmucks* at Cartoon Network produced more episodes of this one than FOX has done of "The Simpsons"!

"They made a whole show about us, that won Emmys and Peabodys and all that, and they didn't even *tell* us about it. Probably did it with hidden cameras and microphones and stuff like that that Allen Funt did on "Candid Camera" back in the day. That's the only way this could have happened." She flipped the brick over to show us the back. "And here's the best part. Top drawer talent all the way! I mean, the executive producers *alone* are Craig McCracken, Rob Renzetti, Seth Macfarlane, Genndy Tartakovsky, Joe Murray, Butch Hartman, Dan Povenmire, Swampy Marsh, Dave Cooper, Johnny Ryan, Alex Hirsch, Lauren Faust, Rebecca Sugar, C.H. Greenblatt, Thurop Van Orman, Tom Ruegger and *STEVEN SPIELBERG*!"

"Good heavens!" said Cerberus, very pleased. "That's practically *everybody* who's *anybody* in television animation right now. We are BLESSED!"

"When the cheques start coming in," continued PB, "we'll be even more blessed in *another* way."

"The *CHEQUES*?" I barked, incredulously. "You mean you'd actually let people PAY you for doing your *job* like that?"

I had good reason to do that. What is a cheque but a piece of paper that guarantees that you will be paid a sum of *money* in exchange for it when you take it to the bank or put it in an ATM? *Money*! And these were the same ladies who only *hours* ago thought capitalism a farcical con game!

The hypocrisy! No *wonder* I was mad.

"We have to get paid *somehow*," said Muscle Girl to me, like I was an idiot who didn't know what a cheque was for. "Licensing a fictional character or a real person's name, likeness and image is how all the money they use to fund their products' development. Why should they not pay us when they pay the rest of their employees for doing *their* jobs? They're all getting *rich* on us, OT. Don't you think we *deserve* a cut of that? At the very *least*?"

"You can't just *squander* your *reputations* like this," I snapped. "Not like THIS! These people represent *everything* you *despise* about the world. EVERYTHING!"

"Squander, nothing!" Candy retorted. "We'd be doing that if we put our names and images on a bunch of things that wasn't WORTHY of having them on it. But this isn't it, Olivia. This crap is all *top of the line*. We got it *all* here. Shirts, pants, dresses, bed-sheets, iPhone covers, ringtones, condoms. The WHOLE LOT! And, if these people are any way the *fair* and *honest* business people that they no doubt are, we WILL be PAID!"

"We take a *lot of knocks* in our jobs," the Brat continued. "There's no guarantee that *any* of us will survive into middle age at the rate we live and work! But look at who I'm talking to. You mortal kids have it plenty easier than us because you can grow up without people WANTING and NEEDING YOUR HELP every MINUTE of the DAY! You'd know that for *sure* if you were one of *us*!"

"If....I was...." Once again, I was outraged. "You did *NOT just* say that. You did *NOT*!"

"We *deserve* to have an annuity to support us doing our "jobs" for no money and little glory all this time!" PB growled. "If I had *two* incomes going for me, instead of just the lousy one I got pumping the keys of my laptop all day right now back home, I'd be able to live in a HOUSE of my OWN for *once* in my life! I'm sure the rest of us could say the same. Why do you knock yourself out protecting the world all day if they expect you to do it for FREE? Besides: you're just *jealous* of what we got now, Thrift. 'Cause you'll *never* have it for *yourself*!"

"Yeah," Cerberus concurred, in a mean-girl tone. "*Jealous* much?"

That was IT!

Nobody insults Olivia Thrift like that- as Captain Fantastic or otherwise. NOBODY! Even *superheroes*. And even if they were my personal *idols*. Emphasis, in that moment, on "were".

So they wanted to be paid, huh?

I'd pay them *back*. With INTEREST!

Chapter Seven: The Pep Talk

"ENOUGH!!!!!"

That one word thundered out of my mouth like a jet of flame from a flame thrower. I wanted their undivided attention to do what I had to do. And I got it.

"*This*," I continued, "has gone FAR ENOUGH! I will *not* allow *any* of you to lower yourselves to the depths of this BARBARITY any further! How DARE you insult the nobility and selflessness inherent in what you do *every day* by allowing yourselves to so blatantly and facetiously be used as mere puppets and *playthings* by *absentee landlords* who don't *care* about you at *all*! Or what you supposedly *stand* for! You *hear* me? You mean absolutely NOTHING to them! And you mean *everything* to me!"

They didn't respond for a moment. They needed that time to comprehend was what being said. The massive amounts of winking and twitching suggested that they were not being used to being lectured to like this, and that they very much resented my treating them like the children some of them were and are. And were as willing to attack me for saying those words as they would if any of their enemies had done so.

But I was as brave and as strong in my thoughts and deeds as any of them. Because they had shown me how to do it themselves. And I knew I had to do what they usually did or said to their enemies to persuade them of the rightness of my argument, as they did with their most formidable foes.

"Come on, Liv," said MG, trying to placate me. "Can't you see that we…?"

"*Get away from me*!" I growled.

So harshly that the otherwise indomitable heroes actually took some steps backwards, for once.

My words were impacting them as I wanted them to. So I kept it up.

I knew that the Merch had brainwashed their minds by putting honey inside of them. Telling them what they wanted to believe about themselves. How popular they thought they were when they weren't. And manifesting everything they wanted to have happened to them in each little trinket they found in this big-box glamour. They wanted to not just be strong and powerful, but also to have economic and social power that had been denied them. They wanted to have all the advantages their superhero peers had been given which had not landed in their laps. Things that only the corporate oligarchies of the American media could give them.

In doing so, my heroines lost exactly the qualities of their personalities that had endeared them to me and so many others. The humility. The responsibility. The intelligence. The chivalry. Everything that separated them mentally from anybody else in both positive and negative ways.

To get them back, I would have to create psychological wounds beneath the surfaces of their powerful bodies. And then rub salt in them. Maybe acid, too. Whatever it took.

I was going to have to tell it like it was to their faces. Insult them severely if I had to. This was the only way to save them, as much as I hated to admit it. They could all kill me easily if they wanted. But I wasn't scared. When I said I knew all about sacrifices, I meant it.

So I let them have it. With both barrels.

"You *dirty* SWINE!" I roared. "You call yourselves *superheroes*? You're *not* heroes right *now*. *You're* PATHETIC! Telling me about how I should yield not to temptation when the bad guys come around, only to start barking like trained seals when there's even a *remote* possibility that some soul-less jackals will come around on a parade float and start throwing *MONEY* at you! What was the *point* of me *literally worshipping* you for most of my life- and I *did,* until NOW- if you're all as *bad* at heart as *any* villain you've fought? Huh? Answer me *that*! What was the *POINT*?"

Tears were starting to stream down my face, and a sob choked my voice, as I spoke. For I hated myself for doing this to them much more than I ever could them themselves. Yet it had to be done, and I did it.

"I admired you all so much," I continued, "that I actually wanted to live the exact same lives you lead. There must be billions of girls who think likewise on Earth alone. How would they feel if they knew what frauds and cowards and impostors you *really* are? Much like me right now. ANGRY!

"You can't have it both ways. *Real* heroines don't need to be in comics or as action figures or on TV shows or other mass-market produced shit that nobody needs. *Needs* are things like food and clothing and personal hygiene you have to have in order to survive. All of *this* is just stuff you *want* to happen to you in the future, if at all. Wants aren't the same as needs. Not everyone can afford to buy all of the things they want. Or even all of the things they *need*, either.

"Because, as much as dreams help us all feel and live better, they can't compete with many of the most difficult realities of the real world. The REAL one. Not the antiseptic pieces of perfection that inconsequential writers and artists make up just so they can feel like their crappy lives have some sort of meaning. No. Not at *all*. The real world is the one you exist in 24-7, and not the one that exist for only a carefully and perfectly executed *half hour* every once in a while.

"Our worlds are those where, when you discovered what great and unique abilities you had, you swore that you always protect them. Even at the cost of your lives. Even at the cost of friends and family if they got in the crossfire. Even the whole planet Earth, or entire galaxies, or the whole universe. Because you knew that, in all the situations you faced, evil was afoot. And you knew that everyone and everything you knew and loved would be in jeopardy, especially if you did *nothing at all* to stop that evil. And more than once, more than I or any other mere mortal human being could conceive of as possible, you did it. You licked the villains and saved the day.

"And you asked for NOTHING IN RETURN!

"This is how things should always WORK in the world. This is how I learned what to value in my life. This is how I learned *exactly* how and when to protect people and things I loved from harm. You weren't the only ones who helped me learn what I needed to know. I know that. But you helped me to do that. A great deal. You can't possibly imagine how often you consoled me when I was depressed or lonely. Down in the dumps. Friendless in both theory *and* practice. Because that's the OTHER way things should always work. You should be able to find encouragement and meaning in the works and deeds of others, whether it be works of art, or crafts like yours, that make you feel like you are not alone by any means in feeling the way you do. And that the world will not harm you any further if you have intelligence, confidence and bravery enough to deal with it as simply and directly as you would another person. Especially when it has done you wrong by any way possible.

"But that ship has SAILED for me when it comes to YOU. Why, it's even run AGROUND on the ROCKS!

"Because, if I can't trust the people I admire the most in the world, who *CAN* I trust? I used to think you were goddesses incarnate. But I know I see you're nothing more than mammon-worshipping *SLUTS*!"

It was starting to work. Their lips started to curl back, revealing their teeth, and they snarled viciously. The actual dog in the group more than anyone. Because no woman- especially not a super-heroine- wants to be called the *other* "s" word.

"Yeah, that's right!" I taunted. "Display for me how *super* you really are! Get mad at me. KILL me! Do what thou wilt! It won't change a damn thing about this even if *you* think it *will*. But go ahead and do it if you think it will *help you*, you back biting, gossiping, cat-calling, double dealing *REPUBLICANS*!"

There. It was that last word that broke the camel's back. Because they, the most progressive and liberal minded people in the universe, hate the people on the political far right for what they've done to the world even *more* than being called dirty anti-feminist names. Which is why I said it!

I got them to listen to me, and reminded them of why it was I admired them. I called them every bad name I knew, to insult them bad enough that they would actually react genuinely and without condescension.

I got them back from the clutches of the Merch then.

But I went too far.

I got them back, all right. But, in doing so, I almost lost my own life. Among the political right, they despise the Republicans most of all, for those Americans among them are the ones who have shown themselves to be the most intolerant and bigoted and repressive of social change when they came to power for over a century. In the process, they killed their famous "dream" of having boundless, unstoppable personal and social success right in its tracks. So saying that they actually *were* of that persuasion, to them, was worse than being accused of sympathizing with the Nazis.

I had never seen such livid hatred in anyone's faces before. And I was potentially on the other side of a worse beating than I even could have gotten at the hands of Gridiron Girl!

With faces showing shades of crimson and purple, they advanced around me quickly, and gave me no possible chance to escape.

Yet, as they did, the glamour of the store disappeared, and we were back on the Merch's ship. I had saved them from their own avarice and greed, even if they weren't yet aware of it.

I was, nevertheless, not harmed, because they were and are merciful in applying their powers when not absolutely required. So, instead of hurting me the worst ways they could, as I feared, they chose instead to speak to me as I had to them, minus the insults. They fought my fire with their own. As they did with their enemies all the time. I turned to face each of them as they spoke to me individually.

"*Strike one,* Olivia!" Muscle Girl warned me. "I don't mind being called names- except THAT one! Try that *again* with me, and you are *out* of my life. And I mean OUT! Understand?"

I nodded.

"*Unnecessary roughness,*" Power Bunny said. "Fifty yard penalty! First down from the goal line. Talk smack to me like that once more and you get *punted* forever! Dig?"

I nodded again.

"*Ten minute major* for MISCONDUCT!" Cerberus roared, after mimicking a hockey referee blowing his whistle with her voice. "*You* go to the PENALTY BOX! Once you've cooled down there, I'll give you another chance. But you'd *better* not do that AGAIN! I mean *specifically* comparing us to the "*Grand Old Party*" for any reason! I think I made myself clear. HAVE I?"

She had, which I indicated with another nod.

The Brat was calmer, since she wasn't yelling at me. But she was still livid.

"The drug test just came back from the words that came out of your mouth just there," she said. "Chemical analysis has determined that it contains trace amounts of provocation, incitement to hatred, and off-the-charts amounts of unjustifiable usage of a tongue! But, as this is your first offense, we are more than prepared to be lenient with you. But be advised that any future trespassing on us in this fashion will not be regarded in the same fashion. Are you prepared to accept these terms fully and without contesting them?"

Nod.

Finally, Candy Girl- who, naturally, seemed the most livid of all of them- spoke. Or, rather, exploded.

"*YELLOW CARD*!" she screamed at me. "Next time, you get the RED one. *Got it*?"

One final nod.

And then, to my surprise, the anger vanished, and they smiled at me contentedly. They were their old ethical selves again. Entirely.

"You didn't think we were *actually* going to lay the *smack* on you, did you, Olivia?" said Muscle Girl, having read my face and mind for the whole time they turned the tables on me. "Nobody deserves that except our enemies. And even though you cussed us really bad there, you're not one of those. You're a *friend*. A really *good* one. Friends should know when other friends are in trouble before they even know it themselves, and the really good ones speak or act up to help them. That's what you just did. Just like Bob and Cerberus both did when I wanted to throw in the towel forever.

"You had an enormous amount of guts doing what you did. Not everyone is even that remotely brave. Especially when they don't have super powers. But I suspect hanging with your pal Captain Fantastic all this time caused some of what she's got to rub off on you."

She winked in a conspiratorial fashion at me, and I returned the gesture.

"Agreed," added Cerberus. "I guess we asked for all of what we got from the Merch *and* you. We're like anyone else in the universe in not wanting to be stuck with what they have and try to find any way possible to improve our position. The Merch found that weak spot in us, and played us like a bunch of Gibson Les Pauls. The only reason we ended up getting out of there- and I mean the ONLY one- was because you, Olivia, were not vulnerable to something we so obviously were. And you let us *know* it. You read us all like a *book*! That whole monologue about what heroism is supposed to represent in our lives and careers was absolutely *inspired*. The insults, not so much, of course. But you blasted the fort with all the guns you had because you had nothing left. And the fort fell *down*!

"You prevented us from succumbing to the most pernicious disease in the universe by reminding us of how honorable we are and are supposed to be, and proved to us that you're a pretty honorable gal yourself. I don't know what would have become if you hadn't done something. We might have become as deranged and mindless as any of the zombies from *The Walking Dead,* and easily kept in indentured servitude for the rest of our days. But that didn't happen, and it won't again. If I have permission to speak for the entire League, we are *entirely* in your DEBT!"

The others said words of agreement. It thrilled me, as you might expect.

"I agree with all of that save for one thing," PB said. "They played us like Fender Strats, not Gibsons. Fenders have a better sound."

"I'm more of an admirer of Rickenbacker," said the Brat. "Especially the twelve string ones. But that's not important. What is important is what you did to and for us, Thrift. You just made it clear that you don't need to be super to be a hero. All you need is to be brave, speak well and direct, and have a mind like a steel trap. You have those things, then you're more untouchable than you would be if you could lift the heaviest thing in the world off the ground. And you *got* it, kid."

"Where have you *been* all this time, Olivia?" Candy exclaimed. "Seriously! That's the kind of cold shower I need to have happen to me all the time when I get so upset I get imprisoned by my feelings, and I can't do a damn thing as a result. I got to do so much of this job by my lonesome, and I spend so much time with my Doubting Thomas brain due to that, and it goes Judas on me whenever it damn well pleases. I can see why some of the supes have *sidekicks* now, because sometimes you just need somebody to *talk* to once in a while. That's why I confide in my brother Finn when nobody else will, and MG talks with Bob, and Cerb' her litter mates, and PB her fellow 'toons, and Brat....whoever it is that she has. Somebody's gotta calm us the F down when we're planning to go on the warpath for no good reason. You did that, and you do it good. Keep it up, and you're really gonna go places."

And then, as if to drop a curtain on this episode, the lights in the room went out.

Chapter Eight: The Hits Just Keep On Coming

It was the kind of all-encompassing darkness you see sometimes in animated cartoons, where the only part of the characters' bodies you can see are their eyes. Fortunately, they knew where I was, and they me, since we remained in place when the lights went off. We thought this would keep us safe.

We were wrong.

It started when Power Bunny reacted with her typical wit to the events by singing what I would later learn was a rhythm and blues song from the 1950s:

"After the lights go down low.

Baby, you know….

They'll be no reason for teasing me so…."

"*Very funny,* PB!" Cerberus said, sarcastically. "This is *not* the time for LEVITY!"

"Yeah," said the Brat. "Here we are, in darkness so deep even we couldn't possibly see through, and *you're* quoting Al Hibbler!"

"Who *was*?" Candy inquired.

"A blind black guy," said PB. "Kind of like Ray Charles, but without the piano. He sang with Duke Ellington before he went solo. And I'm sorry if it seemed like the wrong thing to say, because it felt right. I'm always saying the wrong thing at the right time, or vice versa. It just seemed apropos, considering...."

"Well, it *is* apropos, considering the lyrics you quoted," MG said. "But, having heard that record, I'm of the opinion that Mr. Hibbler was very much wanting his "baby" to make love to him when the lights went down."

"Typical PB," cracked Cerberus. "Somehow, it always comes down to sex with you, doesn't it?"

"Says the girl with no working equipment for that!" PB teased back. "I'm an *adult,* and that's one thing that we adults do in terms of enjoying ourselves. But my life does not *revolve* around...."

She suddenly stopped speaking, and uttered a ghastly shriek.

"*PB*!" we all shouted fearfully, as one.

"What's the matter?" asked Cerberus.

"You have to ASK?" PB squawked. "You, of all people, should know what wrecks me and exactly how it does it!"

"Sure do!" said Cerberus. "I can see it all the way over here. You're on FIRE!"

Fire is the only weakness an animated cartoon character has. The race has filmmaking structure built into its DNA. The earliest ones were made out of film stock containing nitrate, a highly flammable chemical. And many were constructed out of celluloid, a compound that, while durable and flexible, is also vulnerable to fire. This has been passed down the line through their history as a genetic inheritance, and, despite their unique abilities, has always served as their Mark of Cain. And allowed them to be destroyed more easily and capriciously than it should over the years.

So if we didn't act fast…..

"She's going to DIE!" I shouted.

"Not if I can help it!" said Muscle Girl.

In seconds, she had zipped across the room and was next to PB, like a checkmate move in chess. In further seconds, she had grabbed her colleague, laid her on the ground, and coated her with frost created from her breath. In further seconds still, she cracked her out of the frost when it froze into ice.

Power Bunny was alive. But barely. She had been too severely wounded by the flames to be fully alert and active. At that moment, the lights came back on, and we could see all too clearly the exacting scale of how deeply she had been diminished.

"Thanks, Gerda," PB said to Muscle Girl, in a heavily weakened voice. "I owe you!"

Then she became unconscious.

And I screamed.

"It's TRUE!" I shouted. "The Merch know your *weaknesses*! They're using them to try to KILL YOU!"

"You got that right," said the Brat, in a deadly croak years away from her normal healthy robustness.

Those of us still conscious turned to her, and gasped in horror!

The organic parts of her body were weakening. And the mechanical ones were RUSTING!

"The smoke from the flames got in her lungs!" Cerberus concluded. "That's her weak link. First, second or third hand inhaling of smoke. It WRECKS her!"

"You know me all too well, C.," the Brat declared. "But even you guys can't stop this train when it pulls out of the station!"

At which point, she fell over abruptly and collapsed.

And I screamed once more.

"Is there *anything* we can do for them?" I asked the others. "*Anything? At all?*"

"It's not permanent, Olivia," said MG. "If you're worried about them being *dead*, that won't happen."

"They just need some rest," Candy added. "Just like we all do when we get sick."

"But aren't you worried about it happening to you next?" I asked them.

"Of COURSE I am!" said Candy, whose knees began to knock like clicked castanets.

"Stuff!" Cerberus was defiant. "And NONSENSE! The Merch aren't idiots. They know better than try to… OH, *MY GOD! NO!!!!*"

From out of nowhere, a man wearing a white, knee-length lab coat and glasses, and carrying a loaded hypodermic needle, came closing in on us, with his eyes on Cerberus.

"A *VETERINARIAN*!" screeched the Princess of Puppies, in the most astonished, nonplussed and *terrified* tones I had ever heard her speak in. "I'm absolutely POWERLESS to STOP *them*!"

So she ran away, with a cowardice completely foreign to her, as the vet took off in pursuit of her, unmoved. However, even she could not escape the Merch on the move. Or his confederates, it seems. Shortly afterward, we heard a dog- unquestionably her- uttering a long howl begun with defiant anger and rage, yet slowly petering out into the most humiliated whimper I ever heard. They had unquestionably cornered and captured her.

"Not CERBERUS!" I said. "She was perhaps the most inspiring to me of ALL of you, other than you, MG. She was…."

Then I was interrupted by Candy Girl. Who had gone unexpectedly on the warpath!

Her weakness- her own MIND- had betrayed her again, as it so often did. Something or somebody was making her laugh hysterically and driving her to attack us with the beams from her emerald ring.

As if we were ENEMIES and not friends!

"Get *away* from me!" she snarled. "I'm not having any of you parsnips getting anywhere near me! Understand?"

"PARSNIPS?" I asked.

"She's allergic to them," MG explained, as we hit the dirt to avoid her rapid-fire blasts. "Makes her break out in a blotchy rash, and makes her voice almost undistinguishable from a man's. Not as bad as her Benedict Arnold mind, but up there. Thank God hardly anybody eats or sells those things- they mostly grow wild. But it's her mind that's doing this to her. The Merch is fooling around with it like you'd fiddle with the station tuning or volume control on a radio. They're making us think the Earth is under attack from alien parsnips, and she's the only line of defense."

"How can she *possibly* believe that?"

"When you get as crazy as a loon, you'll believe anything you hear. Especially if it's positive in the way that she… LOOK OUT!"

Candy had concentrated much of her ring's energy into forming a giant blast which she now aimed directly at us. I remained on the floor, but Muscle Girl took one for the team. She got right in front of it with her Gibraltar of a chest, and, after a couple of moments of being humbled by the beam, threw it back in Candy's direction. The force of the deflection was enough to knock Candy off her feet and out cold.

I felt like screaming again, but MG spoke before I could do it.

"She'll be fine," she assured me. "She just needs to rest like the…..OH, MY GOD!"

"What?" I asked, alarmed.

"You can't possibly tell, but I can feel the air of my home planet in here now. They saved *me* for *last*!"

As she said that, the most powerful pre-adolescent female in the universe fell straight to her knees. She was becoming helpless rapidly- before my eyes!

"*No,* Gerda!" I pleaded. "Don't let them *do* this to you. I couldn't *stand* it if you did. FIGHT IT!"

"You know as well as I do," she said, as her voice was eroded of its ringing clarity with every word, "that I have absolutely no defense against any of the people or any of the natural resources of my home planet. There was a perfectly good reason why I was physically weak there, as you know, and strong everywhere else. Like I said, the Merch know about me. As much, if not more, than you do. I've been around longer of us than anyone except Cerberus, so they got a whole drawer of a file cabinet about me here somewhere, no doubt. So they're breaking my body now like they just nearly broke my mind. Because they CAN! They're doing this in particular because they know you're my number one fan, and how you saved all of us from that corporate shell-game, so they've decided to humiliate me and sadistically torture you at the same time. But don't let them do it to you like they did us, Olivia. For the time being, this is all in your hands. You have to stop them now. Because we FAILED!"

And, like an ancient and massive tree being felled at last, she collapsed in my arms.

And I screamed even louder and with much more anguish than I had before.

And then I began to cry just as loud.

But the Merch weren't decent enough to leave me alone to cope with the falls of my idols for one second, the JERKS! A group of them swooped in and saw me holding MG, looking like Superman holding the dead body of Supergirl in "Crisis On Infinite Earths".

"There's another one in here," said one of them. "What are we gonna do with her?"

"Have to file a report first," said the guy who was obviously the leader. "They said take down the heroes. But they didn't say the heroes were traveling with any additional goods and services. We'll have to assess its value to see what its' worth is. In the meantime, lock it up, so it can't escape."

"*IT*?" I screamed. "***IT***?"

I didn't even rate being thought of as a HUMAN BEING in their eyes! I wasn't a "she". I was just an item. An "it". We *all* were!

"*HOW DARE* YOU!" I shouted.

But I could do nothing else except shout. For they overpowered and captured me easily.

If I had still been able to become Captain Fantastic, I would have changed at that very moment. But I was simply a normal human girl, who was imprisoned like any other would be in that situation. In chains and manacles.

Effortlessly, I was hustled off and thrown into the nearest jail cell, and warned not to make any noise, or "you're ruined!"

But they were wrong. I wasn't going to be "ruined" at all.

They were.

Chapter Nine: The Big Money

When my captors were no longer in earshot of me, I disobeyed their orders, and loudly started sobbing, like a cruelly abandoned baby. It was all I seemingly had left of me that I hadn't been taken away. My heroines had- astonishing to say - *failed* in their attempt to stop the Merch, and now were locked up like the rest of what they "owned". I myself was being treated no better. They only saw me as a piece of meat not even worthy of being called a "she" or a "her". Somebody who was only worth the dollar sign and the number they probably planned to brand on my forehead.

Such a humiliating end to a day- and, possibly, several lives and careers besides my own- that had begun with such promise and optimism!

There was only one thing left I could do to make things right. And now was as good as any to do it.

It was now or never.

"Lightsound!" I cried out, pitifully. "Are you there, Lightsound? It's me - Olivia! Can you hear me? *Help me! Please!* I'm at the end of my rope here. My powers are gone. My heroines have all been defeated- soundly! I have NOTHING left! Please come down and help me if you can! I never asked a favor of you before like this, but I am now. *LIGHTSOUND*!"

At that point, the Merch guarding me entered the cell and started slapping me in the face to get me to shut up, making me cry out in crippling pain. But that was over almost as soon as it began.

Without warning, my tormentor fell down dead, and Lightsound emerged from out of nowhere.

He was as sympathetic and genteel as ever, just as we had been when we first met, and in spite of the difficult condition I was now in.

"Thank you," I croaked. "I'm surprised you'd still want anything to do with me. After the way I've been carrying on since I lost my confidence and then my powers in one fell swoop, I haven't been useful to anybody anymore. Even myself."

"I would *never* abandon you in your hour of need," he said. "You know that. My race considers loyalty paramount among all the virtues. And, by the standards of *your* race, you are *extremely* loyal. Both to the people who are your friends, and to the fundamental things which you consider important in your life. You demonstrated that very well when you rescued the League from the clutches of the Merch on a mental level, though you could do nothing to stop their physical destruction. If your loyalty had not fueled your drive, things might be far different for you and them."

"It couldn't be any worse than it is *now*," I moaned. "We've all been undone by our weaknesses, including me. And we're about to become mere *property*, instead of the living, thinking and reasoning beings we've always been. The only way to stop it is for you to let me become Captain Fantastic again and use my powers to rescue everyone. If I'd still had them, I might have beaten Gridiron Girl. If I'd found a way to outsmart her instead of slugging it out with her like I did, that is. But if she hadn't deceived me - and *you* - by pretending to be honest and true when she wasn't, she wouldn't have given us all the trouble she did. But maybe that just would have made me just like all the other cocksure asshole superheroes the League *loathes*. I don't know for sure.

"I *have* to become Captain Fantastic again. Whether you like it or not. I became a heroine thanks to you once, Lightsound. Please let me be one again. I promise I won't let you down - like I did *before*."

"I know that," he said. "But it wasn't you who let me down. It was vice versa."

"What are you *talking* about?"

"I removed your powers from you, at the exact moment you needed them. I didn't even see you at the time I did it, because of the way the construction of the city obscured my vantage point. So it was not until later that I learned of how Gridiron Girl had gotten close to killing you with her strength. Although, because she was already stronger than you, that was perhaps inevitable."

"Wait!" Again, I felt the stinging pain of outrage in my soul. "You just LET me get BEATEN UP by the biggest BULLY in the *UNIVERSE*? You let me go through the kind of crippling *pain* and *misery* Dante wouldn't have wished on all the people in *HELL*? Just because you could play *GOD* with me? You SADISTIC *JERK*! I *TRUSTED* you help me stay SAFE through all of this. And now YOU'VE betrayed me, too!"

Then I started crying again.

"There was a good reason why I did what I did," he said, firmly.

"And *what* was THAT?"

"I had determined that the original model of Captain Fantastic was defective, and needed to be replaced. Gridiron Girl became more powerful than you because the manifestation of Jacky Hart's desires was greater than your own. A mass of people, such as the collective players of a sports organization, will always be more physically powerful than any individual could possibly be on their own. And so, I was determined that, if you and she were to fight again, you *had* to be able to have the strength and agility to defeat her. Or at least, show her that you were her physical equal as much as her mental superior.

"So I retired the original model, and set to work devising one that was more suitable to the new challenges you face. You would be faster, stronger and smarter than before. A 2.0 edition, as you Earthlings say.

"Thus, I humbly apologize to you for my actions and all that they caused you. The indignities you and the others endured have been inexcusable. That is more the Merch's fault, of course, but I am also likewise at fault by acting before informing you of my plans beforehand. The good news is, the new model of your illusionary identity Captain Fantastic has now been fully prepared and tested, and is now ready for your full-time application."

"Gosh!" I said. "How stupid am *I*. Flying off the handle like that before letting you explain yourself. I shouldn't have called you those things. They were uncalled for. You had my best interests at heart, after all.

You've been kinder to me than most human beings have! I'd go over there and kiss you- if I didn't have the ol' chains on. That throws a bit of a crimp in your plans. You know as well as I do that I have to jump in the air to activate my powers. How I am I supposed to that with this metal weighing me down?"

"You don't have to jump anymore. That is part of the upgrade. You only need to speak or shout the words now, and it's all fine. Trust me."

"Why in the world would I *not* do that? I do - and I always will. *Always*."

So, taking a deep breath first, I shouted:

"FANTASTIC!"

Olivia Thrift disappeared.

And Captain Fantastic was there in her place. The *new* Captain Fantastic.

I demonstrated my newly regained superhuman strength by ripping apart my chains with power I never had as Olivia. And then I rushed over and embraced Lightsound in gratitude. As I knew I should.

He was right when he said I had been upgraded. Captain Fantastic now wore, instead of the old pyjama suit, a sleek one-piece black swimsuit, like you might see Olympic swimmers and divers wear. It had a stylized "CF" crest on the chest in white, with elongated tails on both letters that coiled them together. On my feet, boots. Not the old ones, of course, but a pair that actually fit my feet snugly.

There was one old thing, though, that was still in place. My blue bicycle helmet. Accompanied this time by elbow and knee pads in the appropriate places. Safety first, after all.

But my body had changed much more than my wardrobe had. My muscles were now as big and powerful as anyone's could become with the proper exercise regimen and no steroids. I felt titanic power coursing through my limbs. My chest and stomach were like the white cliffs of Dover.

No more "magic princess" muscles for me!

And then there was what happened to *my voice*!

I always thought my voice was too high, even as a heroine. We girls all have that problem, even the grown-up women. We have higher vocal registers than men on average, the same as we tend to be shorter and weaker than them physically. It must be our voices that really set most of the men who hate us off. Because, for most of us, that's the only weapon we have against their bullying. We can do things to them - and to *ourselves* - with our voices that they wouldn't dare do even with their fists. If a girl hurts a guy's pride with a well-timed insult, it hurts him even more than if a man said it. Because a lot of them haven't had sisters or aunts or girl cousins, or even mothers, to grow up with, so they don't know how we act and feel in certain situations. Or they've never gone to school with girls at all, and never known how to socialize with them in a mature, non-vindictive way that treats us as their equals and not their inferiors. Which used to be much more commonplace, but is nearly nonexistent now.

And all the boys I know feel the same way. Dixon, for example. His voice is even higher than mine. And that creates the same kind of insecurities. The kind that most men don't have to face after they become men. But

Dixon doesn't let that stand in the way of always treating me like a lady, like the gentlemen he is. If you aren't a prisoner of your hormones, or your stereotypical "interests", you can get a lot of good done in this world.

I say this because my new "hero" voice was not my mousy, weak Olivia voice, but a mighty roar, even when I spoke softly. I slid down the octave bannister from soprano to contralto easily. It was exactly the voice I always thought I should have.

It was so awe inspiring that I actually scared myself saying my first words saying it, thanking Lightsound profusely. He reiterated that it was a pleasure working with me as well, and then vanished.

Once again, I now thought it was possible for me to take on the entire world in a knockout, drag-down street fight if it was necessary to save the entire world from itself. I might have to do exactly that now.

*

I leapt towards the door of the cell, my foot outstretched and a battle cry in my mouth. The door was no match for me. It shattered into splinters, and I was outside, on the floor. Proudly standing up.

To the shock of the first Merch I met in the hallway as I flew down it.

"*HALT*!" I thundered.

He did. And I flew in front of him, like a sergeant dressing down an incompetent private in an army.

"What," I demanded, "have you people done with the International League of Girls with Guns? *And* the Canadian Consortium of Superheroines?"

He was too scared to answer me right away. So I flew in closer, and grabbed his hand with mine.

"You better *tell* me where they *are*!" I ordered. "Or else your hand is going to end up like the door I just busted down. *BROKEN*!"

So he told me. In a very detailed way, as I then insisted he do. Once I had the paper with the instructions from him, I let him go, and went to my destination.

*

I went in by kicking the door down again. Ho-hum.

But what I saw in the room was *not* ho-hum.

Not at all.

The League and the Consortium were all there, as I had been told. But they were stuck inside the kind of giant room-sized tank you'd only find in an aquarium. There wasn't any water inside of it, though. No need. They weren't fish.

But they *were* prisoners.

Alive, yes. And thankful for that as I was, I assume. But still prisoners.

They look completely spent and exhausted. Like drunks locked up and cooling their heads after getting loaded on Saturday night. There was no joy or merriment in their eyes, as I had seen in all of my previous encounters with all of them. The kind that had literally been leaping out of them once. Only *hours* earlier, in fact!

They had, after all, been nearly killed by the only things or people who were capable of doing such. That creates feelings inside of you that are the total opposite of mirth.

But I sympathized with them, entirely. It had happened to me as well, and on the same day. Not at the same time, but in an equally divisive and apocalyptic fashion.

So, if anyone could possibly sympathize with them now, it was me.

I tapped on the glass to let them know I was there. They didn't respond. Initially, I got mad about that snub - until I realized it *wasn't* one. It wasn't their fault. It was the *Merch's*. They made the glass *go one way only*. Anyone looking on the outside could see the inside of the tank clearly, but those inside had their vision and hearing obscured. So they couldn't even know that they were being bought and sold until it was too late to do anything! They wouldn't even be given the choice of living free or dying as slaves!

You think I was going to stand back and let that happen, now that I could do something about it? Oh, no! I WASN'T! I may not have been able to stop them being captured as Olivia Thrift - but *Captain Fantastic* could *easily free* them!

So I didn't hesitate. I raised my right arm up high, and balled my right hand into a fist.

AND SWUNG!

With a very satisfying CRASH, my arm broke through and smashed a huge hole in the feeble glass. I then added to that by super-speed dashing around and creating further huge holes. Within moments, the entire wall of glass was crumbling away into shards.

And my friends, deprived of genuine fresh air for such a long time, took big whiffs of it in their lungs.

And were reborn.

As the powerful super-heroines they were and were meant to be.

With great happy, surprised and ecstatic exclamations in their voices, they surrounded me. Cautiously, as first. Until they realized I was not a foe, but somebody they may have met somewhere, some time before, but couldn't yet place the face or name.

"Howdy, stranger!" Cerberus said. "We sure *owe* you. *Plenty*. But who *are* you?"

"My name," I rumbled triumphantly, "is CAPTAIN FANTASTIC. ***And I AM CANADIAN!***"

If they didn't know me before, they did now. And they liked every bit of me.

*

"Sorry I'm late," I continued, quietly this time. "The Merch figured out how to separate my powers from me same as they did you. So I only just got here. I had to get a new battery for my car."

"You didn't get a new battery, CF," MG corrected me, impressed. "That's a whole new *vehicle* you got there."

"Right from the dealer's showroom," added Candy Girl.

"Not *even*," corrected Cerberus. "That's right off the *assembly line*! Those guns easily qualify you for full membership in our outfit!"

"We better *give* her that, then," added Power Bunny. "This whole thing has me convinced me that we really need to fill out our ranks. Five folks may be enough for your average rock-and-roll band, but you need a lot more than that to fight evil. We might need the odd ringer to help us once in a while, like Cerb' was saying about the sixth man before."

"Not just *her*, if we're gonna be fair about it," the Brat said, as she gestured to the Consortium. "We gotta take all of *them*, too."

The Canadian girls really thought that was boss, given the smiles they had on their faces then.

"You need big numbers to fight big battles, after all," the Brat continued. "That's what the DC and Marvel crowds have been doing all this time, and apparently, it works. If we're the U.S. Army, they can just as well be our National Guard. At least in Canada, because they know that place better than the back of their hands."

"I have absolutely no opposition to that," said Muscle Girl, in her mightiest take-no-prisoners voice. "*Whatsoever*. However, we still have more important things to deal with here."

"Yes," Cerberus sliced in, also back on her game. "While the Merch is still around, we haven't done our job yet. But no worries there. Especially considering what PB and I learned during our earlier confinement apart from the rest of you by accident. In QUARANTINE!"

"*Quarantine*?" Candy asked. "Don't they just do that if you're a foreign species entering a new place?"

"What do you think we are to *them*?" PB grated. "They poked and prodded me like I was a *circus freak*! Just 'cause we happen to be so-called "dumb animals", they think...."

"Please!" Cerberus cut her off. "You just got off with being BURNT a little bit! *I*, on the other hand, got pumped full of so many drugs that I was higher than *The Grateful Dead* was for most of the *1960s*! If I'd simply been mortal, I'd be DEAD! If there was no such thing in the world as medicine, my race would not suffer as much...."

"Don't *go* there, Cerb'!" Candy cut *her* off, in turn. "I'd be as loony as an English village idiot without my meds!"

"That's not what she meant, Candy," I said, in a mediator's tone. "Animals get forced to get well or better in a way humans aren't. Some veterinarians are terrible about forcing them to take shots for diseases that they may never get. And the way they treat animals who can't be classified as pets is worse, because they apparently think they won't make any money treating them. I- or, I should say, *Olivia* - once took an injured bird to one of my local ones, and the very first thing he said about it was that it needed to be put down!"

"Let's cut out the bitching, okay?" MG said, with some annoyance. "That's not going to solve any of our problems right now, and we all know it. But if Cerb' and PB learned anything from their quarantine experience, they better share it with us."

"Which we *planned* to do *anyway*," said Cerberus. "Gather 'round and we'll tell you. But don't make too much noise. The walls in this place really have *ears*."

So we gathered 'round.

*

Once briefed, we headed out of the room *en masse*, as confident a group of soldiers of virtue as you might find anywhere. We were unopposed by all except a few of the more foolhardy Merch who tried to stop us, and we disarmed them easily with our powers.

Our destination was the massive conference room that occupied the center of the ship, where the Merch held their business meetings. They happened to have planned to have one just as we converged on it. Fortunately for us.

We came to a collective stop quickly in front of the entrance to the room. Where a short, fat and balding man resembling a penguin with no feathers or beak sat snoring, loudly. The blood of us who were Canadian turned ice cold, for we all knew *exactly* who he was.

"*Tabernache*!" Superflic exclaimed, in a harsh whisper. "Michael Dufferin! That *cochon*!"

"Who *is* he?" said Candy, who, being American, had never heard of him. "And what is he to *you*?"

"He's a Senator," I said. "Back in Canada. Or he *was*, anyway. They drummed him out for not doing his taxes the right way."

"Not the kind of guy I would have voted for, then," Candy retorted. "If I *could*."

"Nobody *votes* for Senators in Canada, Candy," Muscle Girl said. "That particular chamber is full of people who were *appointed* to it. By the Prime Minister. In this case, the most *evil* one we ever had!"

"That's not unlike the situation in the House of Lords in England," Cerberus observed. "Same problems there. Wealthy and entitled people engaged in so-called 'sober second thought' on the people's dimes."

"Not like your American ones are any better," the Angel of the Tar Sands reminded us.

"No d-uh," said PB. "But the *Romans* started all of that mess. Not one of their *better* ideas!"

"But at least them Americans gets voted out of office once in a while," said the Newfie Bullet.

"*Ours,* in contrast," the Raven snarled, "get put in there for *LIFE*! Or, at least, 'til they reach retirement age. It's only once in a blue moon they take punishment action like they did for Dufferin. And that's more to get rid of the really bad apples among them than clean things up for *real*."

"I've dealt with him and his cronies before," said Muscle Girl. "Let me deal with him."

She marched up close to his face.

"*DUFFERIN*!" she barked.

The man sprung awake. And then he recoiled in horror.

"DAMN IT!" he said. "You got *out*. *All* of you tramps got OUT!"

"***TRAMPS***?"

He sprung back even more quickly than before when we said that together.

Because you don't call *any* respectable lady a "tramp" without hearing about it from them. In *that* context, it doesn't mean "hobo".

We were all livid. But not so much as the one who was actually speaking to him.

"*You,*" Muscle Girl roared, "better *open* that *door* RIGHT NOW, you *slime-ball*! And make sure you tell your *lords and masters* that we are here to *see them* RIGHT NOW! And, for that matter, let him know EXACTLY how we feel about being treated as OBJECTS and not PEOPLE! ***AND WE WILL BE HEARD!***"

"Please!" He got down and begged in front of her. "Don't do that! I'm in enough trouble as it is…"

"We don't CARE!" MG grated. "Open the door, and *stay out of our way* after you do it. OR ELSE!"

So he opened the door for us without another word. We went into the inner chamber.

However, we soon discovered we had been tricked. The room we thought was past the door we entered and the one nearest us was *not* the door into the board room *at all*. The board room was *below* our feet, enclosed by a floor made of glass that served as its ceiling.

A glass ceiling was literally keeping us out!

"One door?" said Dufferin, cryptically and rhetorically. "No, ladies! There are *two* doors! You got me to open one of 'em by opening your fat mouths, but the old Duffster don't get fooled twice by the same dumb kids. No, sir!"

And with that, he went out of the room, and *locked* us in it.

Fortunately, we were locked in at an appropriate place at an appropriate moment.

They- all of them men- were entering the room for their conference at that moment.

And, boy, did we get *mad*! Even more than we were earlier!

We actually knew who all of them were. More than that, we *despised* them all, collectively and individually. We'd encountered and bested them in previous encounters all over the universe. But, because of their wealth and influence, they had not even been punished remotely for any of their misdeeds. They'd all lived to fight another day after they had fought and then run away screaming from all of us.

Stephen Hotspur, the aforementioned ex-Prime Minister of Canada, sat at the head of the table with a gavel in his hand, as the chair. His grey-helmeted hair and bespectacled face cast the same sort of unfeeling glare he always had as the Baron of Ottawa, and perfectly indicated how his inability to sympathize with anyone who was in the way of what he wanted and desired had gotten him his job. To his extreme right was Roland J. Crump, the millionaire American realtor, then in the midst of a heated campaign for the Presidential nomination of our loathed Republican party. Crump was even worse than Hotspur, who had least had some women in his Cabinet, in that Crump used women only for personal hedonistic urges, and thought they were not worth anything to him or anyone else otherwise. He had even less use for those people from minority groups, and based his campaign on making them the chief and erroneous scapegoat for the nation's current problems. What threw us a real curve was that Crump's main rival for the nomination was sitting opposite him at the other side of the table. Senator T.B. Sheets of Texas was a bigoted evangelical Christian who thought less of minorities of any kind than Crump did. The massive gold crucifix he wore around his neck, as a symbol of his faith, cast such a glare in the light that it nearly blinded us when he leaned forward.

Besides them, those in the know recognized the chairmen, CEOs, CFOs and presidents of nearly every company involved in every business in the world, considering how many of them were now folded into each other. In protective, unaccountable wombs, like the insides of Russian nesting dolls. The major Canadian ones were there, of course, which got the Canucks' goats. Many of them had tried to use economic leverage to gain unfair socioeconomic advantages in our home towns. And thanks to us, they had, at least temporarily, failed.

We were unquestionably mad. As you would be in the same situation, no doubt.

For how would *you* like it if you worked as hard as you could at your job, and did the best job you could considering your social, personal and economic circumstances, only to have your work totally and completely *undone* every chance your opponents could take advantage of you? And, if, despite most of your best efforts, and the incredible resources you had, you were unable to prevent them from doing it AGAIN? And then AGAIN *AFTER THAT*?

It got worse than that, if that can be believed, when Hotspur banged the gavel and they began speaking.

About *us*!

Without us *there*!

And without us even having a voice in what was going to be done with us!

We weren't going to *stand* for it. Not anymore.

We started yelling at them and taunting them, hoping that, unlike the glass in the aquarium tank, they *could* see and hear us above them.

"You *idiots*!" said the Brat.

"Come up *here* and say your *sexist* crap!" I roared.

"You are DEAD if I catch you, Hotspur!" declared MG.

"Will you be MAN enough to speak about us like that when we're in the ROOM, CRUMP?" said Power Bunny.

"I can almost SMELL you, T.B. Sheets!" growled Candy.

"You PIMPS!" said Cerberus. "We are NOT your *HOOKERS*! I don't know about the rest of you, but I done had ENOUGH of this!"

She breathed in, and uncorked a sonic bark even louder than any one any of us had been on the other side of. The reverberations completely destroyed the glass, and the floor-cum-ceiling crumbled beneath us, causing to fall down into the conference room. Much to the shock and surprise of the men, who apparently couldn't see us or hear us at all, given their reactions.

"Damn it, Nigel!" Hotspur said accusingly to his secretary, at the opposite end of the table from him.

"You *specifically* told me that that glass was *unbreakable*!"

"It *should* have been, Steve," Nigel said. "That's what the salesman said when I bought it. I paid $90,000 for it. Guess I got gypped."

"Probably was a bitch like them who sold it to him," observed Roland Crump. "Most of what them Janes want from you is your money. Maybe your body, but nothing else. Usually it's money."

"The *pot* can't call the *kettle black*, pal!" Muscle Girl warned him. "Now, how about you hardened cons let us know where your real bosses in the Merch are?"

"You're *looking* at them," said Hotspur, bluntly.

The ladies in the room gasped.

"We *are* the Merch," Hotspur continued. "And we always *have* been."

"Well," said Power Bunny cheekily. "*That* explains more than a *few* things about you all."

"Who, exactly, do you think has been *running* things on your planet all this time, friends?" Hotspur asked, rhetorically. "People who look like us. *Exactly* like us. This has made it considerably easier for us to blend in with you and take over than it would have been any other way. Our ancestors first started colonizing your lands in the period you call the Industrial Revolution, and we used our abilities to harness natural and other resources and create vast amounts of wealth from them to our obvious advantage. Your endless ability to consume conspicuously, coupled with the decline in the fortunes of your organized religions…"

"Speak for *yourself!*" interrupted a resentful T.B. Sheets.

"...made you putty in our hands," concluded Hotspur.

"But it's getting hard out there, now," Roland Crump said. "The white guys who were *not* Merch - and there's *plenty* of them, too - made it plenty hard for us back in the day when they let you dames start *voting*. You liked having that little bit of power you never had before too much for your own good, and you haven't shut up about *righteous* you are since. Complaining loudly about every little thing we do like you never did bad yourself. Flaunting yourselves around Earth like ya *owned* the place. Well, you don't. We *do*."

"The worst aspect of *that* particular problem," added T.B. Sheets, glaring venomously at the Raven in particular, "is that your particularly feminist brand of "social activism" has utterly convinced too many of those whom the Bible clearly designates as *inferior* beings that rebelling against their *betters* is the only way to achieve the damnable "change" and "justice" and "peace" they keep saying they want. The *lower races* demanding their so-called "civil rights" is bad enough. But now they have been joined by further abominations in the form of those who covet the bodies of the same gender as themselves, and those who utterly *refuse* to accept that Earthly vessel to which *God Himself* has assigned...."

"CRAM IT, SHEETS!" Candy roared, slapping him in the face so hard he was knocked completely out of his chair. "That *act* of yours may play well in the STICKS, but not with *us*. I was too merciful letting you live the last time. I should have *broken* your miserable *neck*."

"That, however," said Cerberus, "is where we *differ* from the likes of *you*. We believe in goodness and mercy, where *you* do *not*. Your businesses, regardless of what you actually SELL, is making *money*. Hoarding unneeded merchandise, and selling it to anyone who can afford your highway robbery prices. And you even do it for the *fun* of it sometimes."

"I refuse to respond to that on the grounds that it may incriminate…" one of the CEOs began.

"*SHUT UP*!" I shouted at him. He did.

"But you gals are in business, too," said Crump. "In a way of speaking."

"*Excuse me*?" said an insulted Muscle Girl, rhetorically.

"Roland has a point," Hotspur added. "You operate on a model in which you provide your services to those who need them at times appropriate to both them and you. That's similar to how any other normal business operates. The only difference is that you are not paid a salary for doing your job, nor do you accept payment for your work of any kind. But you can give what you have to provide and take it away as any other business person can. Therefore, you are not in any position to tell us how to do our jobs. At least, not until you figure out how to do yours on a financially *profitable* basis."

MG knocked Hotspur's glasses completely off his face with one swipe for that one. Then she grabbed the labels of his jacket and stared directed into his naked eyes with her own.

"Don't you dare!" she said. "Don't you DARE compare yourselves to US! You have no *right* to make that comparison- under ANY CIRCUMSTANCES!

"Maybe you have a point from your end, but we have a superior one on ours. We happen to be in a business that does *not* concern itself with filthy lucre or pleasures of the flesh. We are beings dedicated to improving the world through our actions as much, if not more, than you are to DESTROYING it! There, our paths differ. But then they *converge*. Much more than any of us want."

She released her grip on him, and began addressing all of us instead.

"None of you men think of yourselves as 'villains'. Because you believe you can justify and account for your actions the same as we can ours. And because that allows you to justify the very flawed ways in which you live your lives the way we do ours as well. Yet even our *enemies* know *who* we are, and plot their plots against us based on those reasons. You aren't even *men* enough to give us that singular COURTESY!

"You don't even see your victims as living beings at all. All they are to you is numbers on one of your LEDGERS! Well, get this. Every time you try to fool around with the numbers on those ledgers- like, say, to make them BIGGER - actual *people* and *places* get *hurt*. In the *worst possible ways*!"

She cast her eyes back on Hotspur, who had retrieved and replaced his glasses in the interim.

"Now, as *you* used to say in *your old business*, SIR," she said, "we are taking you and the rest of you spineless, cowardly bastards and *throwing you under the bus*!"

Turning to us, she issued a sharp, direct command:

"GET 'EM!"

Like we needed to be encouraged.

The next few minutes were a blur. We literally tore the room apart. We destroyed the rich wood panelling in the walls, and the expensive paintings and sculptures all around and near them. We upended the men from their expensive leather chairs and smashed the chairs to bits, threatening the men on them into silence by implying we'd do the same to them if they cracked wise. We reduced the massive conference table to smithereens, and ripped the plush carpeting beneath it out of the floor it had been installed in. When we finished with that, the room was as bare and Spartan as the giant jail some of us had only recently been confined in.

The men themselves we treated little better. We grabbed the carafes of hot coffee and cold ice water placed on the table, and threw them over their heads and down their pants, delighting in the shock and agony they felt. Our fists and legs connected well and often with their faces and crotches. The Raven, in bird form, began pecking and clawing at them in hopes of tearing out their eyes. If they wore toupees to hide growing baldness, those were unceremoniously removed violently. I myself was greatly pleased to discover that the vainglorious Roland Crump wore one such item, and, therefore, I delighted myself in relieving him of it.

Cerberus in particular was in her element, having had her dignity and pride as a good and honest dog more deeply stolen from her than of all of the rest of us combined, not to mention her very life. She spent much of her time eyeing the men like a wolf would a shepherd's flock, and occasionally her mighty jaws bit so hard on a man's exposed hand or leg that the crunch of breaking bone was heavily and sickeningly heard throughout the room. But her masterstroke came at the end, when she cornered Hotspur's flunky secretary, Nigel White, and, while levitating in the air like some sort of Buddhist deity, mesmerised him with her all-mighty mind.

"*You*," she ordered, "will gather every bit of flammable material you can find, and place them all in the EXACT spot on this pathetic *tub* where it can do the most *damage*. *Then*, you are to get items by which you are to start the greatest conflagration you or anyone else has ever seen. Kerosene. Matches. Cigarette lighters. Rocket fuel. Pixie dust. Whale oil. *Something*. I don't care. Just *go*. Do *exactly* as I command you, you sycophantic *fool*. And don't spend $90,000 doing it, *either*!"

Nigel went out of the room, without saying anything. Not even "Yes, ma'am". He was as willing to thoughtlessly follow her orders to the letter as he no doubt had Hotspur's all those years before.

"This is a suicide pact!" Hotspur now said in response. "You don't realize that this ship is made out of the cheapest building materials that were available to us. Fire will *wreck* it!"

"Not to mention me," said PB, casting a cautious eye at the flying dog after disposing of a victim with one of her famous carrot-shaped beams of light.

"*You* have *nothing to worry about*," Cerberus responded. "By the time Nigel gets the Guy Fawkes Day bonfire going, we'll be *gone*. We're pretty much *done* here as it *is*. So let's BLOW this joint!"

"Then let me put the first *nail* in the *coffin*," said Muscle Girl, as she magnificently lifted Hotspur up in the air by the collar of his suit jacket. Then, like a quarterback throwing a forward pass, she threw him across the room and through the wall, where he landed noiselessly. The rest of us got the picture, and did the same with a victim of our choice, until they were all out of the room and out cold.

At which point, smoke started coming through the holes in the wall.

"Darn!" the Brat cursed. "Not *again*!" She flew out of the room, in the opposite direction from the smoke's path.

"Wow!" said Cerberus. "That Nigel sure is efficient. I thought it was gonna take him HOURS to start a good blaze! If he wasn't such an evil guy, we could've used him as *our* secretary. Or at least, *I* could as *mine*. I'm so dumb with keeping track of my life sometimes."

"Let's get out of here before I *flame* on!" Power Bunny said. "And then *you* all do, too!"

So we did, with those being able to fly carting those who couldn't under their arms like they were so many handbags or purses. We followed the way the Brat had gone, and she met us out there, unharmed and safe as we all ended up being.

The ship exploded soon after, like a supernova.

And there was no question in our mind that no one could have survived an explosion of the enormous magnitude it proved to be.

Even though, in space, nobody can hear you die.

Chapter Ten: The Epilogue

And you want to know the *weirdest* thing about it all?

It wasn't even 5 o'clock yet when we got back to Winnipeg, and the grounds of the Millennium Library. Mom was still going to be able to pick me up on *time*!

We were just in time to get a couple of special phone calls, which the League answered for us via their private joint line. First came the Suckerpunch Girls, our absent friends and idols, direct from their very home and *room*!

Thankfully, the kerfuffle with Moving Drawings that had grounded them had now been settled out of court. The whole affair had been executed by their despised nemesis, Lady Warbucks, who had induced her wealthy father- a Merch, though he wasn't one of the guys we saw on the ship- to purchase majority control of MD's parent company, Timely Warmer, so that the inferior version of their program- to be produced as cheap stick-figure drawings rather than the lavishness we and they were used to- could get a spot on the air without the execs being able to say what a piece of crap it was, even if they *wanted* to. Unfortunately for Lady, her dad ran afoul of the Federal Communications Commission, who ruled the intended takeover was a blatant conflict of interest given his prominent investments in other media concerns, and they killed the deal dead. So the series never even got produced, and the lawsuit the Girls launched to protect their good names died with it.

The greatest thing, though, was that they knew what we had just done. And even better- they were PROUD of us for doing it!

The Merch ship going up was visible right from their flight path as they were coming home from court. The residue of it remained in the sky there- and presumably was visible from every other vantage point like that in the world- for over an hour. And they got what happened. Immediately. Despite their enemies' claims to the contrary, they're not idiots by any means. Just like we aren't.

They, and so many of the other heroes and heroines that they're pals with, had been gunning to take down the Merch the very moment they made their presence felt where they were based. They told us that themselves. And also, in getting rid of them ourselves, we had, in the process, relieved them and the rest of the world's heroes of the biggest burden that ever could have been placed on them.

If you thought that we second-stringers weren't pleased to hear *that,* you would be *mistaken*. It was all the validation for our work that we needed to hear!

They promised to make it up to us sooner rather than later, and signed off.

At which point, we were then rung up by the Prime Minister of Canada himself.

Not the *late Right Honourable Mr. Hotspur,* obviously.

It was his successor. His more honorable, just and *handsome* successor, the *Right* Honourable Jeremy Thibodeaux. If you get my meaning there.

He had seen the explosion in the skies over Ottawa as he was leaving his residence, and immediately had to figure out what was going on. But he liked it when he found out what happened, since he's a Liberal, and he hates the Conservatives more than even the Canadians among us do. E*specially* when he found out the nationality of the majority of the heroines who had done the deed!

"We need more of your kind of people in Canada," he said, between about a bajillion annoying glottal stops. "No. Make that the *world*. What we *don't* need is the kind of excesses my now deceased predecessor clearly exercised as part of his reign of error. Good job!"

He promised we'd be received in style like the heroines we were the next time we were where the Ottawa, Rideau and Gatineau rivers met, and signed off.

That was even better than what the Girls said. Because there's nothing can make any sane girl go *insane* better than a handsome man complementing you in any way possible! Especially when a dreamboat like *him* does it. Even Cerberus was perking up when she heard him, and she's *sterile*!

"I wish he was a bachelor!" Candy said. She spoke for *all* of us.

Then we all had to split, sadly. The League members went off to their own lives and affairs, and the Consortium went back to the Marlborough to prepare for their individual journeys home.

Soon it was just me and Muscle Girl- or, should I say, Gerda- left.

"Remember," she said, after one more affectionate hug, "any time you need help- any time at all- call me and tell me what you want. And if I'm not up to my panties in trouble myself, I'll come running. But mind you, *no crying wolf*. That's when you get the other strike I warned you about. I have no time for thoughtlessness, as you know."

"Understood," I replied. "I'm the same, as you know. I have no time for thoughtlessness, either. So whatever you said goes double for me. I owe you too much."

"I owe you the same," she said. "See you 'round, Olivia."

And she took off into the air, back to her small town home up north in the Interlake region. And then was gone.

I then said "Done!", and went back to being Olivia Thrift. Just when my Mom showed up, thankfully.

We exchanged pleasantries, but when she asked how it was, I just said "fine". And she let it go at that.

I can't afford to let her know what I am, and what I can do. Not for *anything*. After what I went through, I know what it's like to nearly lose everything in your life that really matters. And I'll be damned if I allow it to happen to me again.

But I can't wait until I let my cousin Ella know all about this. I'm saving it until the next time she comes out from Vancouver, so I can see and hear her reaction right in person.

She is going to be so *jealous*!

Author's Bio:

David Perlmutter is a freelance writer based in Winnipeg, Manitoba, Canada. He is the author of America Toons In: A History of Television Animation (McFarland and Co.), The Singular Adventures Of Jefferson Ball (Chupa Cabra House), The Pups (Booklocker.com), Certain Private Conversations and Other Stories (Aurora Publishing) Orthicon; or, the History of a Bad Idea (Linkville Press, forthcoming), and The Encyclopedia of American Animated Cartoon Series (Rowman and Littlefield, forthcoming.) He can be reached on Facebook at David Perlmutter-Writer, Twitter at @DKPLJW1, and Tumblr at The Musings of David Perlmutter (yesdavidperlmutterfan).

CPSIA information can be obtained
at www.ICGtesting.com
Printed in the USA
LVHW042350261119
638675LV00018B/804/P

9 781988 827339